A Gathering of Ghosts

There seemed no reason why the planning application to take over run-down Rampton's Farm and build a leisure complex in its stead should not go through smoothly—until Arnold Landon from the planning department visited the site. For Arnold was a man who understood wood, and the timber-framed building revealed to his discerning eye unmistakable evidence that it was unique in the Northumbrian countryside.

But at the meeting of the planning committee Arnold found himself vigorously opposed by Professor Fisher, a university medievalist who swore the barn was later in date, of a common type, and not worth a preservation order. Revisiting the barn to check on the information it had vouchsafed to him, Arnold found that an interested party had also revisited it—and had not left it alive.

The barn was slow to yield its secrets, but Arnold's persistence in the end won through. The old building revealed not only its history but the secret for which someone had been prepared to kill. As its ghosts gather, it becomes clear to the police and to Arnold Landon who the murderer is.

ROY LEWIS

A Gathering of
Ghosts

First published 1982
by Wm. Collins Sons & Co. Ltd.

This edition published 1986
by TOTEM CRIME
a division of Collins Publishers
100 Lesmill Road, Don Mills, Ontario

Canadian Cataloguing in Publication Data

Lewis, Roy, 1933-
   A gathering of ghosts

ISBN 0-00-223113-1

I. Title

PR6062.E954G3 1986   823'.914   C86-093730-5

Printed and bound in Canada.

Ghost, n. The outward and visible sign of an inward fear.
Ambrose Bierce: *The Devil's Dictionary*

CHAPTER 1

1

The Senior Planning Officer possessed a range and colour of expletive that was beyond Arnold Landon's comprehension. Arnold presumed it was the direct result of the Senior Planning Officer's flirtation, when young and immature, with the engineering industry, where he had learned all about such mysteries as male and female joints before he was tempted by the precise delights of cartography and the mediaeval excitements of architecture. But they had been the formative years for the Senior Planning Officer and they had overscored his verbal elegance with an occasional uncontrollable coarseness, exacerbated by tension and the realization that at five-thirty he would be faced with his wife's Thursday cottage pie. He hated cottage pie. He had once confided this to Arnold. It was a confidence Arnold had always respected.

For Arnold admired the Senior Planning Officer. He admired his lean, grey-suited form, the coolness he normally displayed at planning enquiries, the panache with which he dealt with philistinism from ignorant councillors and greed from property developers. He had once devastated a Secretary of State in front of his own Departmental Inspector. And he had had the foresight to realize that Arnold Landon had been wasting his time in the Town Clerk's Department. For that fact alone, Arnold admired him and would forgive him anything, even his language when he lapsed from good taste, as now.

'It will be boring,' the Senior Planning Officer had warned him. 'And frustrating.'

But not to Arnold. The move to Planning had been a
dream come true, for it had brought him into contact
with the world of reality, his reality; and it had given him
the opportunity to indulge his passion.

The expletives gradually died away and the Senior Planning Officer, tapping his fingers on the desk in front of
him, leaned back in his chair and shook his head in mock
despair. He never indulged in real despair: that was
reserved for the dark hours of Friday mornings when the
tiger growled desperately in his stomach and indigestion
burned off the reason in his brain. 'This,' he said snap-
pishly, 'is going to be a real swine, Arnold. I feel it in my
bones.'

Arnold had a respect for the Senior Planning Officer's
bones: they sometimes told him things that were denied
lesser men who lacked such sensitive structural
foundations. 'I feel it in my bones,' was precisely what he
had said when he had appointed Arnold to his department, so Arnold was bound to respect such impressive
judgments. After all, Arnold had had no formal
education that fitted him for work in Planning: a passion
for woodwork at school had left him relegated to the non-
academic stream, and though he had considered he had a
certain artistic flair for a possible career in technical
drawing and design, the death of his father had necessitated early employment for Arnold, and that had meant
a job as a clerk in local government after the war. Eight
years of drudgery in the Town Clerk's Department had
been ended only when, through some process of osmosis
the details of which he still only vaguely understood, the
information had percolated to the Senior Planning
Officer that there was a queer chap in the Town Clerk's
Department who seemed to know absolutely everything
there was to know about wood, and building materials,
and odd things like that. There had been an historic,

albeit accidental meeting among the lunch debris in the canteen, when the Senior Planning Officer's bones had become amazingly operative. He had told Arnold, after two hours' discussion, that he had learned more about the historic buildings of Northumberland in that two hours than he had gleaned in thirty years' scouting the hills and fells, and wouldn't Arnold consider a transfer?

Arnold would, did, and was transferred.

His consequent happiness, and respect for that first perceptive judgment, now made him wait with unabated respect for the Senior Planning Officer's comments.

'It's going to have all the features of a real squabble,' the Senior Planning Officer said, steepling his fingers thoughtfully and caressing his ginger moustache with his thumb. 'I had dealings with Mr Rampton—old Fred Rampton—some years ago and it's an experience I occasionally recall with feelings far from nostalgic. He's a sour old bastard.'

'His farm—'

'Is just beyond Whinsill. Close to the Cumbrian border. It's a considerable pity, in my view, that the border raiders never succeeded in annexing that whole stretch of countryside to Scotland. It would have saved us the headache of this planning application at least.'

'What exactly is the difficulty?' Arnold asked.

The Senior Planning Officer unsteepled his fingers and gestured towards the manila folder on the desk in front of him. 'You'll find it all there, in detail. But, baldly, the situation is this. We have an application from Mr Rampton for agreement to a change of user in respect of his farmlands. It's a change that is designed to bring our revered chairman of the Planning Committee, Colonel Summers, that much closer to the apoplectic fit we have feared and his good lady has dreamed of for years. There will be a militaristic bark of defiance from the Colonel, an insistence that we fight to the last ditch in this battle, and

thereafter a committed press campaign which will make
our work doubly difficult as the protectors of our heritage
line up fearlessly to fight those who would look to the
developing potential of the north-east as a tourist area.
We, my dear Arnold, will be called upon to provide the
ammunition for both sides, and you know precisely what
happens to ammunition carriers in any war.'

Arnold knew. They got shot at. At a nod from the
Senior Planning Officer he picked up the manila file and
took it back to his office. He, it was clear, was to be
ammunition carrier in chief.

But all stormy days had their beauty: there were sunsets,
the fresh smell of rain-soaked heather, the high roaring
thrust of the wind on a fell. The file lay before him and he
read it, but without the sense of despair that afflicted the
Senior Planning Officer. He could see the problems in it,
understand the planning complications, be aware of the
political struggles that would blind the committee
members to the basic merits of whatever cases he and the
Senior Planning Officer might put forward. But he could
not summon the sense of despair that duty and loyalty
towards the Senior Planning Officer might have
demanded.

Frederick Rampton of Rampton Farm was making
planning application for a change of user, prior to sale of
his lands, in respect of the farm. Side by side, there was
the document prepared by the solicitors to Brandling
Leisure Pursuits, and the supporting planning
application and appropriate affidavits and plans,
outlining the proposal made by the company and
incorporating Rampton Farm, which had obviously led to
Fred Rampton asking for change of user. Fred Rampton
stood to make a lot of money out of the planning
application if it succeeded. So, presumably, did
Brandling Leisure Pursuits. And Colonel Summers would

sneer and raise his bloodshot eyes to the ceiling of the
Planning Committee Room and call down upon the
applicants, silently, the wrath of the cherubs that
disported on what he had been heard to describe as the
'Muriel' there. Colonel Summers had no time for culture.
Nor for anyone who wished to despoil his beloved
Northumberland. Particularly that part which bordered
upon Cumbria and which hosted some of the best rough
shooting in the north and was rented by the Colonel's
county friends.

It would be a bitter fight, and a nasty one. But not,
perhaps, a long one for the relevant Planning Committee
would be only a fortnight away. It meant some swift work
for Arnold. But he despaired neither for that, nor for the
bitterness of the projected battle. For this file would
transport him out of the office, and across the ploughed
fields, over the farmlands so that he would be able to
recall yet again the long summer walks his father had
taken him on, through tiny Yorkshire hamlets, deep in
the dales, where the air was broad and fresh and singing
in his lungs and he could live, and feel, and remember.

Within the hour he was on the road across country
from Morpeth to the Cumbrian border.

Cumbria was not Yorkshire, of course, but it was little
different from Northumberland and with this last county
Arnold had fallen in love. It possessed a great deal of the
boyhood magic he had experienced but the particular
grandeur of its wild, sweeping hills had the capacity to
snatch the breath from his mouth on occasions. And it
held an advantage over the countryside of his childhood:
it was almost littered with the detritus of history. It
seemed that no matter where Arnold turned, no matter
where his job took him, there would be something fascinating for him to look at, investigate, consider at his leisure
away from the office. It could be a crumbling wall, or the

ruins of an old pele tower; a tumbledown farmhouse or a
decayed farm wagon; the carvings on an ancient door
lintel or the handworked pews in a thirteenth-century
church, nestling under the rounded, tree-banked slopes
of the northern forestland. Escape from the office was
important because it cast Arnold into the delights of the
countryside as it was doing now, and he drove westward,
looping towards the uncompromising directness of the
Roman road with an uplifted spirit.

The bones of the Senior Planning Officer might ache
with ill-omened anxiety, but for Arnold there was the
excitement of a new location.

West of Hexham he turned northward, driving deep
into the land beyond the Wall, a wild folded land that
had seen the marauders of centuries thrusting across its
rich earth. He had already consulted his map carefully so
he had no need to consult it now; it meant he was able to
devote all his attention to the harsh stark beauty of the
countryside about him. He had phoned Fred Rampton
from the office but had been unable to contact him: his
nephew, one James Rampton, had given Arnold the
necessary permissions so Arnold was free to roam the
farmlands, and undertake what surveys he deemed necessary and the Senior Planning Officer required to ease his
tensions.

Armed with his notebook, Arnold spent the long morning walking across the fields, noting boundaries, checking
on views and locations. The farmlands were extensive,
bounded to the north by another farm overshadowed by a
broad clump of trees, but there was a decaying, unhappy
air about them as though they lacked the husbandry and
sense of purpose the rich earth deserved. The farm itself
nestled in a hollow at the end of a track winding along a
narrow valley, one and a half miles from the main road:
picturesque, it nevertheless reminded Arnold of the dying
Yorkshire Dales of the 'thirties which had brought such

old village had a written history, one similar perhaps to
Ford, the Northumberland village razed by the lady of
the manor because it spoiled her view to the hills above
her estate. But even as he wandered, enjoying the feel of
the hill, a slight uneasiness prickled the back of Arnold's
neck. His mind was not entirely upon the enjoyment of his
discovery. Something bothered him, something concerned him. A light breeze had arisen with the
lengthening shadows and it might have been the cool
touch of that air, but he felt it was really due to something else. There was a *presence* near by, something that
had little to do with the shadows beneath his feet, under
the tussocky grass, buried and all forgotten.

There was something else, and the heritage of his
father whispered to him. Arnold lifted his head and
looked about him.

The Old Wheat Barn.

The breeze rose again, soughing softly over the long
grass. Arnold walked towards the old, leaning structure
and it rose out of the slope of the hill as though to greet
him. But he walked almost reluctantly. He had a feeling
about the place, a suspicion that it was peopled, alive, the
kind of feeling he sometimes had about old buildings, a
feeling he almost feared because of the intensity it could
create within him. An intensity, a longing to know, when
the knowledge, finally, was always impossible to obtain,
for the ancient walls could not speak and the windows
were blind, the doors gaping holes into the past.

Arnold stood at the wide doors and looked up above
him to where the sturdy, repaired roof was stark against
the sharp blue of the sky. He hesitated, almost fearful, for
he felt the shiver again, the shiver he had only occasionally experienced but which always presaged excitement and discovery. But inside, there was nothing.

At least, not at first.

He walked into the ancient barn and it had the decay

of the Rampton Farm generally. Its age gave it no protection from the sourness of the farmlands below: there
was an atmosphere of staleness and disuse inside the barn
that saddened Arnold, the way the sight of an old work-
horse grazing its days away blindly saddened him. And
yet, in a little while, something began to change within
the old barn. Arnold looked up, his eyes becoming
accustomed to the dimness of the light and the roof
seemed to take on the arching height of a cathedral, the
aged rafters curving away into a black obscurity, as the
dust danced in shafted sunlight to the earthen floor.
Perhaps it was the sympathetic presence of Arnold himself that brought the old barn back to a living existence:
perhaps its old timbers responded to the stored knowledge
and appreciation of his fingertips and eyes. The walls
began to creak lightly to him, the rafters groaned with a
soft sighing sound as though to tell him of the load they
had borne for a hundred years and would continue to
bear for long beyond his lifetime. But not, Arnold
thought, if the planning application of Brandling Leisure
Pursuits is approved.

Above him the rafters groaned again, uncomprehending.

Arnold walked back into the fading sunlight. He
looked at the map, consulted the survey notes he had
made, riffled through some of the details of the planning
application once again, and then turned to look down the
hill towards Fred Rampton's farm.

That was the way it would be. There would be no place
for this old barn if Fred Rampton sold out to the
Brandling Group. It would have to go. All it had resisted
by way of weather and man's neglect would be as forgotten as that village buried under the hillside, once the
developers came thrusting across the farm, creating
adventure playgrounds, roads, a zoo and the services for
the camping site and pony-trekking stables that would

form part of the Brandling complex.

The old barn would have to go.

The thought of the cost of progress distressed him. With deliberation Arnold turned his back on the barn and walked down the hillside, away from Fred Rampton's farm, and towards the roadway. From the map, it seemed it swung around on the border of the Rampton land, abutted on the adjoining farm, and would eventually emerge about half a mile from where Arnold had left his car.

He crossed the meadow, giving not a backward glance to the doomed barn above him, climbed over the stile and dropped down into the narrow roadway beyond. He began to walk back towards his car, beyond the hill.

He had walked perhaps three hundred yards when he heard the muted roar behind him. It changed to a chugging and he looked back: a tractor was coming along the road, pulling behind it a wagon on which had been loaded newly cut green timber from the clump on the hill. Arnold walked on and then, as the tractor drew near, he stepped aside, standing awkwardly astride the ditch to allow the vehicle to pass.

The driver flicked a quick, uninterested glance in his direction. He was middle-aged, with saturnine features and a dark-stubbled chin that seemed to sit well with his general air of dissatisfaction. He drove the tractor with an air of determination as though he wished to bend either machine or roadway to his will. He would, Arnold considered, be a man to whom all life was a problem and a bitterness. His attention turned to the second man, seated on the wagon behind the driver.

Arnold's scrutiny was returned. The man on the wagon would be seeing in Arnold a lean middle-aged man with thinning, greying hair, a windburned face from which a nose like weathered timber projected above a wispy, ineffectual moustache. Arnold found himself staring at a typical Northumberland farmer: broad-shouldered in his dark sweater, leather-elbowed; a craggy face marked and lined by eroding outdoor years; eyes blue with the far-away look that could be the result of wide horizons or a lost past, and the gumbooted solidity of a man who had made a successful life doing what he liked doing.

The tractor rumbled past, and the man still stared at Arnold. Then, as Arnold stepped back into the road, the farmer tapped the driver on the shoulder and said something to him. The tractor slowed, stopped, and the farmer looked back towards Arnold. He waited until Arnold drew near, and then he smiled.

'You want a lift?'

2

Arnold hesitated.

The farmer looked back over his shoulder and gestured with a lift of his chin towards the road looping over the hill. 'That's three-quarters of a mile and it can take the legs out of you.'

Arnold was persuaded. He took advantage of the helping hand held out to him and stepped up to sit opposite the farmer on the edge of the wagon. He clutched his document case to his chest as the driver cast a sour glance in his direction before starting the tractor on its way.

The farmer grinned vaguely at Arnold.

'Don't often see people out this way,' he said. 'A few walkers from time to time. Hikers, like. But not many others.'

His eyes drifted an enquiring glance towards the document case, the enquiry emphasizing the incongruity of such appurtenances in the Northumberland countryside.

'I work for the Planning Department,' Arnold offered lamely.

'Planning?'

Arnold was aware that the farming community had reason to feel from time to time that the bureaucracy of planning cast a blight upon their activity: there were occasions when he had been made to feel cast in the role of saviour by some beleaguered son of the soil but such instances were stalks in a field of wheat: most of the time, planning officials were classified along with barn pests that crept out of the hay at night and sucked chicken eggs with rodent teeth.

'I've been undertaking some survey work on the Rampton Farm,' Arnold felt constrained to say, defensively.

The farmer looked at him not unsympathetically and nodded. 'Oh, aye. My neighbour. His land abuts on mine.'

He turned his head away so Arnold could no longer see his eyes. The man's head was leonine in profile, the grey wiry hair a shaggy mane, his features strong and determined and experienced. But as he suddenly turned his head again to face Arnold there was a fleeting expression, a shadow that was left briefly exposed that seemed to denote uncertainties behind the strength. 'My name's Ben Kelvin. You know Newman Farm?' Arnold nodded: he had seen it named on the map. 'That's mine,' Kelvin added with an air of satisfaction. 'Farmed it for almost forty years, now.' He paused, pursing his lips. 'Good farming land: always destined for farming land. And I've *worked* it.' There was almost a challenge in the words, but Arnold could see no reason for the aggression. He waited.

Ben Kelvin stared moodily around him at the hedges and then jerked his head towards the driver. 'This is Jack Sorrell. Used to farm down along those meadows.

Worked for me ten years now.'

Sorrell did not turn his head but there was resentment in the line of his back. There was no way of knowing whether he was resentful because he had lost his farm, or because he did not like being reminded he was an employee. Or maybe he was touched with that primitive superstition that held a man was in a stranger's power if that stranger learned his name.

Kelvin seemed unaware of the resentment. He stared briefly at Arnold and then leaned forward, bowing his head, his eyes half closed. He seemed almost to be praying for a moment, but Arnold guessed that Kelvin, now his curiosity about the stranger was satisfied, had nothing more to say and was probably even regretting the invitation he had extended in the roadway.

Next moment Ben Kelvin surprised him again.

'You'll work from Morpeth. Fair drive, end of the day. There'll be tea ready at Newman Farm.'

Arnold's surprise led him to accept the invitation.

Jack Sorrell dropped them at the end of the lane and then proceeded on towards a cluster of outhouses some fifty yards away. Ben Kelvin strode slightly ahead of Arnold, along the muddy lane marked by car tracks towards the warm brown stone of the farmhouse that lay at the end of the track. The farmhouse lacked the natural form Arnold associated with such functional buildings. The left wing of the structure was gabled in a subdued, mock-Gothic style that was completely out of harmony with the central block of the building: that, Arnold suspected from its steady squareness and no-nonsense look, could well date from about 1700. That part of the farmhouse which received the swing of the lane was much more recent, however; it was likely it would have been constructed at the turn of the century or just before the First World War. Perhaps there was something in his silent scrutiny of the buildings that was communicated to Ben Kelvin for he grunted and lifted his head, gesturing towards the farmhouse. 'The Newmans have lived and worked on this farm for two hundred years but they always had more money than sense.'

Not quite right, Arnold thought: more money than taste.

And when he entered the main living area of the farmhouse his view was confirmed, because though the Newmans may well have lacked taste, there was a common sense displayed in the interior of the house that appealed to Arnold. Functional but comfortable; homely but direct. Heavy timbers that would have outlasted generations; a generous use of good sound timber in the construction; the warmth of old, well-tried furniture of a traditional kind — which would now be worth a small fortune in an auction room — and overall an impression of depth and solidity and stability.

'My wife will be resting,' Kelvin said. 'She's not too well.'

'I'm sorry to hear that. Perhaps I should not have—'

'Kitty'll be bringing in the tea. No bother. My wife may be down, but she gets back trouble and spends most time in bed.' Kelvin waved a hand towards a deep leather armchair. 'Sit you down.'

Kitty, who proved to be a small, homely woman of indeterminate age, materialized in a few minutes with a tray and some sandwiches as though she had been expecting the visitor. Kelvin attacked the sandwiches without inhibition, though Arnold suspected they would be merely a prelude to a heavier meal later in the evening. He was feeling somewhat peckish himself so he took a couple of the ham sandwiches and, in the face of Kelvin's munching silence, looked approvingly around the room.

'East wing of the farmhouse,' Kelvin said suddenly, 'it was built to provide for the larger Newman family that came traipsing in from Norfolk. Not much used now, of course, since there's just me and Alison. She was an only daughter, you see, and we've had no kids ourselves.'

There might have been just the shade of regret in Kelvin's tone so Arnold said hurriedly, 'The west wing's a lot older, though, isn't it? Mid-Victorian, I would have thought. And this part we're sitting in, my guess is it would have been the original farmhouse, built around 1700.'

'Dare say you might be right.' Kelvin took a sip of tea. 'One wall at the back of the house, that could be older. Alison once told me she reckoned it was maybe a hundred years older than this bit. You interested in that sort of thing, then?'

Arnold lifted a deprecating shoulder. How could one adequately explain to a stranger the overriding and peculiar passions of one's life? 'I have an . . . interest,' he said. 'Though I'm really more concerned with the timbers that—' He broke off as Kelvin's glance caught his.

'You'll not be up at Rampton Farm to look at old buildings, though,' Kelvin asserted.

'Well, no—'

'Planning Department, you said.' Kelvin nodded to himself, as though confirming he had indeed heard the words. 'You'll have been up there, looking around, because of Rampton's big ideas.'

'Big ideas?'

'His planning application. I seen a copy. When it was put up for objections.'

'You objected?'

'I did.' Kelvin glowered at his teacup. 'That's farmland down there. Good farmland too: I know it. All right, it's gone bad these last ten years and more but that was old Fred's doing. He never did come to grips with that land. He never saw sense the way I did, here at Newman Farm. This is a bigger place, but it could have gone downhill just like Fred's if I hadn't had the sense to realize I couldn't handle it all by meself. First, I got a young feller from the university. He came in with some good ideas, and I gave him the chance to put it all into practice. By the time he wanted to be away, get a place of his own, he'd set me on the right road, with cycles, markets, machinery, stock, everything it takes to make a farm work and bring in profits. He gave me the chance to see what was possible, and I'm a quick learner. So, when he was gone, I had the lessons, could apply the system — and all I needed then was practical help.'

'That's where Mr Sorrell came in?'

Kelvin flashed him a sharp glance. 'That's right. Jack had lost his farm — result of a quarrel with Fred Rampton if you want to know. He needed a job, he's a local man, so . . . I took him on.' He seemed about to say more, but then lapsed into silence.

Arnold finished his tea. It was time he was going. He was on the point of saying so when Ben Kelvin said, 'So what about this planning application, then?'

'How do you mean?'

'Will it go through the Planning Committee?'

'I really can't say. I'm merely one of the officers who—'

'Hey, come on,' Kelvin said testily, 'I know it's the councillor members of the committee who'll be making the decision, but I also know that they're bound to be guided by statements made by you Planning men.'

'I'm not sure—'

'So what'll you be saying about the application?'

Arnold slowly rose to his feet. 'It's a bit early to be making any judgments, Mr Kelvin. I've only just undertaken a preliminary survey. I've got my notes to write up, and then I'll have to come back to make certain other inspections—'

'But have you got all the facts?' Kelvin said sharply.

'I'm not sure I understand what you mean,' Arnold

replied, unable to keep the frigid note out of his voice.

Ben Kelvin rose, shook his leonine head. His eyes were flecked with a slow resentment, inexplicable to Arnold. There was something else there in their depths too, but hidden and controlled, even from Ben Kelvin himself perhaps. So many men could be strangers to their own motives: wood was an honest material that could bring a man down to basic patterns of life, and Arnold felt the simplicity of his own emotional and mental state was due to his lifelong passion for wood. Kelvin would be a more complicated character—but then, so were most men, compared to Arnold Landon.

'Come here,' Ben Kelvin ordered and strode out of the room into another, broader room at the front of the farmhouse, overlooking the front yard and giving a view of the tree-clumped hill, the ancient barn just below the skyline, and beyond, the range of the Northumberland hills, fading blue into the distance. 'Look,' Kelvin insisted. Arnold looked, understanding. Out there was some of the finest farming land in the country—not merely because of the richness of its soil or the grandeur of its location, but because of the same sense of isolation, of being, of living within and being part of the environment that some of the Yorkshire dales could breed in a man. The planning application that nestled within the manila file would change all that and perhaps destroy that close-grained isolation. It was of a different world and it came from a different world where values were different, needs were different—and where the profits of life were measured in financial terms rather than in all those ways which Arnold and, it seemed, Ben Kelvin knew about. Yes, Arnold understood, and needed no explanation from Kelvin. But, at the same time, it was not his decision.

'You'll have strong support from the Chairman of the Planning Committee,' Arnold offered.

'Colonel Summers?' There was a note of derision in Kelvin's voice. 'He'll go about things the wrong way. Oh, he'll oppose Fred Rampton's scheme all right, but he'll see it as a damned war, and when wars start people get bloodied and sometimes the wrong side wins. The winners in *that* kind of engagement are the ones who can buy the bullets and the troops. And the money is going to be lying with those who'll be pushing this scheme.'

Arnold guessed he was probably right, even though he himself would not have been so sure. Environmental matters had a way of arousing great passions in people, and moving them to great deeds. 'Well, I really had better be making my way back to Morpeth—'

'How much exactly do you *know* about this application?' Kelvin demanded, returning to the theme he had earlier embarked upon.

'My brief—'

'Does it tell you aught about the parties behind Fred Rampton?'

'The application is supported and, I suppose, financed by a Newcastle-based group called Brandling Leisure Pursuits.'

Ben Kelvin smiled thinly, the deep lines around his mouth accentuated grimly by the lack of mirth in his smile. 'Brandling Leisure Pursuits. Sounds real open-air, doesn't it? As open-air as the kind of pleasures they want to set up for white-faced city folk out here among the hills. But do you know what most of their work covers?'

'I'm afraid I have no background information on the company since at this stage it is no part of my—'

'One-armed bandits; pool halls; night clubs; red light districts in Sunderland and Middlesbrough; on-course betting at Newcastle, Wetherby and Thirsk . . . anything, in fact, which is just this side of legitimate or which can't be handled by the police with the kind of proof they need.'

'Are you serious?'

Kelvin glared out at the landscape beyond his farm and nodded. 'I'm serious.'

Arnold considered, eyeing Ben Kelvin thoughtfully. 'I'm not sure that the committee will necessarily take this into account, but I suppose all the facts ought to be made available to them.'

'Damn right,' Kelvin agreed. 'And they better take them into account, too, because if there ever was a doubtful organization it's that bloody Brandling Pursuits mob.'

'I'm not sure you—'

'Listen.' Kelvin turned to look directly at Arnold and his mouth was twisted, his tone low but urgent. 'As soon as this planning application came up I took the trouble to start getting the facts about the whole shooting match. The company was only set up about three years ago, and it arose out of the kind of widespread operation I just mentioned to you. It was spawned in the north in 1971, and it grew like a weed, you know what I mean? The boom among the working men's clubs gave the group the foothold they were looking for and they spread throughout the north-east.'

'Foothold?'

Kelvin nodded. 'That's right. They're not northerners— not the controllers, at least, though they employ enough Newcastle musclemen to call it a local firm now. No, they came up from down south, when the going got too hot for them down there.'

Arnold scratched his cheek nervously. 'You're telling me the company consists of people from the . . . the London underworld?'

Ben Kelvin's glance suggested scorn for Arnold Landon's naïvety. 'You never heard of Charles Burke?'

Arnold's main interest in life did not extend to reading the popular press nor to following the reports of criminal behaviour in either the north or the south. He shook his head. Ben Kelvin grunted. 'Well, you'd better get his name down in that document case of yours.'

'He's involved in Brandling Pursuits; is that what you mean?'

Kelvin shook his head. 'Not *involved* with them. He *is* Brandling Pursuits.'

'So who is he?'

'Not the sort of character I'd want for a neighbour, that's for sure,' Kelvin replied emphatically. 'He's a Londoner—East-Ender, I think, originally, but he struggled up out of that background and he now affects an Oxford accent and country tweeds, with a large house at Corbridge complete with paddock and all the trimmings and a string of legitimate-sounding activities through a series of company directorships. But leopards don't change their spots.'

'What kind of . . . ah . . . spots does Mr Burke possess?' Arnold asked nervously.

'I don't know too much about his background from his London days, except that it was distinctly shady.' Ben Kelvin gnawed at his lower lip for a moment. 'You see, when this application came up I thought I'd better make some enquiries and I got in touch with a firm in Newcastle who did some checking. They pulled Charles Burke's name out of the hat, and since I'd already heard of him I asked them to dig a bit deeper. They eventually produced a file for me. Interesting reading, it made.'

'Interesting?'

'Clever man, Mr Burke. Or lucky. Couple of charges for fraud against him in his early days but he had either good lawyers, or good accountants. But there was pressure, so he came north. Moved into the working men's clubs with a one-armed bandit organization, and then moved outwards from there. Bought a few councillors, the whisper goes, made a few bob in the building trade, but his main income was from his fringe industries—and they were definitely

West End stuff.'

Arnold wrinkled his brow. His memory was stirring. 'I'm not sure . . . it seems to me I might have heard his name . . .'

'I'd be surprised if you hadn't,' Kelvin said sourly. 'It made all the newspapers at the time.'

'What did?'

'The Scotswood Murder.'

Arnold remembered. A body found in the Tyne, north of the Scotswood Bridge. The man was local, came from Gateshead, but had been acting as a bookie's runner in the West End of Newcastle. He had died from strangulation, but he had been tortured before he died: his fingertips had been burned and there were burns also on other parts of his body. Sensitive parts, Arnold recalled with a shudder. 'I don't remember the details . . .'

'Gangland killing,' Kelvin said shortly. 'The man had been bilking his bosses, and had salted away a few thousand on his own account. He was quite a tearaway lad, but he was too stupid to realize it was dangerous to try to put one over on the club bosses. They made an example of him. But they were careless too: when the body was fished out of the Tyne there was a ticket discovered in one of his pockets. It was a racing slip, but it had a few names scribbled on the back. One of them was Charles Burke.'

'I don't remember Burke ever being arraigned, even though there was talk —'

'That's right. Prominent Northern Businessman Held for Questioning, that sort of newspaper chatter.' Kelvin nodded. 'Aye, he was questioned all right, but he talked his way out of any involvement, or his lawyers did, anyway. And they never did fix on anyone for that killing — but there's an awful lot of people consider Charles Burke was behind it all.'

'And this is the man behind the planning application.'

'That's the way of it,' Kelvin said shortly. He turned away again to stare out over the fields to the wood-clumped hill and the blue sky beyond. He was silent for a little while, until Arnold shuffled uncomfortably.

'I'm grateful for the information, Mr Kelvin, and the tea. But I'd better be on my way, now.'

Kelvin turned and led the way out of the farmhouse to the yard. He stood there, burly, his mouth set in a grim line and Arnold paused, hesitated. 'I'm not sure whether what you've told me is relevant to the planning committee deliberations. Hearsay . . . but even so, I'll make some further enquiries of my own. On the other hand . . . have you said anything about this to Mr Rampton?'

Ben Kelvin smiled, but the smile did nothing to relieve the grimness of his mouth. He shook his head. 'Ah, Fred Rampton. Aye, I told Fred. Asked him, in view of the kind of man he'd be selling out to, and the damage the scheme could do to the environment around here, whether he wouldn't reconsider. Made him an offer for the farm, in fact. Turned me down flat.'

'Your offer presumably wouldn't have matched that of Brandling Pursuits.'

'Right. My offer was based on agricultural prices, plus a bit more. From Brandling, lot bigger. Development ideas. But that wasn't the reason for his turning me down.'

'A neighbour—'

'Doesn't have to be a friend,' Kelvin interrupted starkly. "You met Fred yet?"

Arnold shook his head. 'I shall probably be calling on him tomorrow.'

'You'll make your own judgment then. But Fred and me . . . well, it's long ago now, but grudges stick with Fred. And maybe he resents the way I've improved this farm, while his has drifted downwards. No matter. Main thing, for me, is that this planning application don't go through.' His eyes drifted back, almost involuntarily, to the hill. Then his glance snapped back to Arnold. He seemed to consider for a moment, and then he said, 'You seemed interested in the farmhouse here.'

'I find old buildings interesting. The construction—'

'Maybe you'd like to call back some time, take a look at the older section that Alison's always on about.'

Somewhat taken aback, Arnold began, 'Well, I—'

'Any time. Next week maybe. Call around when you've been down at Rampton's farm, and you're welcome to take a look around.'

And as he walked along the track, making his way back to his car, Arnold was still vaguely puzzled, although pleased. Ben Kelvin's sociability surprised him: farmers tended not to welcome planning officers. Unless they wanted something from them.

And in this case Arnold could guess what that something was.

3

The Senior Planning Officer was not happy and announced the fact.

'I should get the survey completed by Tuesday,' Arnold said helpfully, 'and half of the documentation for the committee is already complete.'

'Complications.'

'I beg your pardon, sir?'

'This Burke business, Arnold. I don't like it. Planning matters, they should have *clean* lines. Issues should be direct, clearly identified. If this Burke thing comes up there could be problems. I suggest we should bury it.'

Arnold thought of the sweep of the hill above Newman Farm and the possibility of gangland thugs setting up pleasure operations on that hill. He opened his mouth, then closed it again. He had been about to say something unprofessional. His business was facts, not comment.

'You were about to say something, Arnold.'

Perceptive as ever, Arnold thought. 'Only about to agree with you, sir.'

The Senior Planning Officer allowed satisfaction to creep into his voice. 'Yes . . . we'll have to play down the Burke involvement. After all, the man's . . . ah . . . notoriety has little or nothing to do with the facts placed upon the application by Mr Rampton. Rumours and scandal . . . they have no place in the atmosphere of a planning committee: clinical, Arnold, that's what it should be like. Clinical.' He savoured the word silently, moving his lips to the sound. 'When will you be completing the survey, Arnold?'

'Tomorrow morning, sir.'

'You will be seeing Mr Rampton?'

'At ten.'

'Well, keep it clinical, Arnold.' He fixed Arnold with a sharp eye. 'Don't get *involved*, now, will you? Maintain a professional . . . ah . . . detachment.'

The Senior Planning Officer always maintained a professional detachment. It was why Arnold's desk was often inundated with papers he would have expected the Senior Planning Officer to have dealt with.

The following morning the skies were grey, leaden-hued with the threat of rain. Arnold drove west to complete the survey of Rampton Farm and the surrounding area: if he could finish the survey, as he had promised the Senior Planning Officer, it would mean he could easily complete the supporting papers for the meeting of the Planning Committee the following week. That would please the Senior Planning Officer, and incidentally give Arnold time to wander around the Ogle churchyard for a couple of hours at the weekend.

Arnold was a little early for his appointment with Fred Rampton so he stopped the car on the ridge overlooking the farmlands and got out to stretch his legs. There was a coolness in the air that suggested rain was not far off, and in the distance the hills were magnified to his vision, a trick of the moisture in the air. He stared down at the farm: squat, ugly buildings sprawled around a littered yard. The windows were shuttered, the roof in need of some repair and there was an air of general neglect about the place that compared badly with the Newman Farm over the hill. A couple of scrawny dogs rooted around in the yard; the barn doors seemed to be hanging at an angle suggestive of disuse, and the track that led down to the farm in the hollow was rutted badly and in need of repair. The farmlands were sour, uncared for, the land of a farmer who had lost interest, or inclination, or mere heart.

Arnold drove down to the farm in sombre mood.

He had once walked in Swaledale with his father and he had seen tears in his eyes at the destruction of a way of life, then. Rampton Farm would not raise in Arnold's breast that kind of reaction: the place was such that it seemed never to have become part of the landscape, never to have been part of the agricultural community. It was like a scar on the landscape, a forgotten backwater that had never been protected, cosseted, made to bloom and flower, and so it had probably always been in a state of decay. But the thought was fanciful: all this atrophy could have been the result of one bad husbandman.

The man who answered the door to Arnold's knock was tall, broad-shouldered and fair-haired. He was about forty years old with a thin-lipped mouth that would rarely smile and eyes that held an innate suspicion that would rarely be relieved. His clothes sagged on him, ill-cut, careless, and his shirt cuffs were ragged and worn. He was far from welcoming.

'Who're you?'

'My name's Landon. From the Planning Department. I have an appointment with Mr Fred Rampton.'

'Oh, aye. We spoke on the phone the other day. I'm James Rampton.' He made no attempt to extend his hand. After a short pause in which he looked Arnold up and down he evidently deemed him harmless and jerked his thumb over his shoulder. 'The old man's out in the kitchen, at back.'

Arnold followed the reluctant invitation and as James Rampton led the way along a flagged passageway that smelled vaguely of boiled cabbage, he glanced about him, noting the state of the walls, the damp of the wallpaper, and the general sad air of decay. The kitchen was broad, generous in proportions but filthy in state.

'You Landon?'

'Mr Rampton?'

'That's me.' The owner of Rampton Farm scowled at Arnold belligerently. He was perhaps six feet in height and unbowed; about sixty years of age, he still held himself well, but though his body might be strong and healthy his craggy face showed the destruction that dissatisfaction could wreak upon a man. His eyelids were heavy and disillusioned; the wide mouth had a turned down appearance and the sag of his weatherbeaten cheeks denoted a reluctance to accept that life had anything good to savour. Fred Rampton might well have been defeated by the farm; perhaps he had defeated the farm. Arnold suspected he would never know, for whatever it was that had killed something inside Fred Rampton it would have been so long ago that maybe no one now remembered — merely saw and felt the decay of man and farm.

'You come to finish the survey? James tells me you was up here the other day, up on the hill.'

'That's right, Mr Rampton. I needed to walk the

boundaries, carry out certain checks with regard to the environment—'

'What the hell for? Straightforward, isn't it?'

'Not quite, Mr Rampton. You see, the interests of other parties abutting on to your land must be taken into account—'

'Rubbish! My land; my application. Nothing to do with anyone else.'

'That's not quite how the Planning Committee sees things. They have a duty to consider such matters as environmental damage, the rights of other landowners in the area, the likely impact of the planning scheme you are putting forward and the—'

'Adjoining landowners,' Fred Rampton interrupted suspiciously. 'You mean they got a say at the committee?'

'Well, to a certain extent. Their views—'

'That'll include Ben Kelvin?'

'As one of the adjoining owners—'

'You already seen him?'

Arnold had the feeling he was not playing a full part in the conversation. The Senior Planning Officer would not have approved. 'Mr Rampton,' Arnold said, clutching his document case with commendable firmness. 'I think I'd better explain things to you. I have to provide all the facts relating to this application to the Planning Committee. The committee will need to take into account a whole range of relevant factors. One factor will be the impact the development scheme would make upon agriculture in the area. And since Mr Kelvin has lodged an objection to the scheme it is inevitable that his views will be sought, and his arguments investigated.'

'Bastard.'

Arnold was not certain whether the remark was directed to himself or the unavailable Mr Kelvin; he decided to regard it as a comment directed towards the latter. He glanced back over his shoulder. James

Rampton was standing in the doorway, arms folded, gaze fixed on the fireplace. He seemed hardly to be listening. Arnold took a deep breath. 'Anyway—' he began.

'No. You lissen to me.' Fred Rampton stepped closer; there was the reek of stale onions on his breath. He raised a hand, the argumentative finger was stained and black-nailed. 'This is my land; my farm. I been here a long time, and my mother and father before me. *My* farm. If what I want to do with it is farm it—my business. If what I want, for the good of me, and my nephew here, is to sell it to someone—my business. And if I want to sell it to someone who ain't going to farm it, but use it for something else—my business, and his business.' He moved a step closer and his rheumy eyes grew dark with anger. 'And as for that bastard over the hill, let me tell you something. I'll never let him dictate to me the way I'll run my life or my land. He can do what he wants over there on his wife's bloody land; he can bring in fancy notions and newfangled ideas if he wants, but I'll have the last laugh on him because I'll make a profit out of this land that he'd never match in two lifetimes, and he'll have no bloody say in it! I'll see him in his grave first!'

'I'm afraid you don't understand—'

'I understand, Landon, understand only too damned well. Now you better understand. If Kelvin's got any idea of upsetting my planning application he can think again. I'm not having that bastard run my affairs. And you can stick *that* in your report!'

Arnold had the distinct feeling he was not getting very far. The tip of his long prow of a nose would be getting pink with embarrassment, he knew. He cleared his throat. 'All right, Mr Rampton, I accept the . . . ah . . . point you're making but it's one I can't really pursue right now. Can I just ask you a couple of questions regarding the change of user application first . . . ?'

They spent ten minutes dealing with some of the fac-

tual statements made by Fred Rampton and in the
supporting documents provided by Brandling Leisure
Pursuits; as they talked Arnold was aware of the presence
of James Rampton brooding in the background. He had
the feeling that while the nephew was perfectly in accord
with his uncle's plans, he was at the same time uneasy
about something. Maybe it was Fred Rampton's attitude
of open belligerence that disturbed him. It certainly
disturbed Arnold.

When the interview drew to its surly conclusion Arnold
gathered up his papers and prepared to leave to complete
the survey of the farm boundaries. Casually, but with a
dry mouth, he asked: 'Have you had any other dealings
with Brandling Leisure Pursuits, Mr Rampton?'

Fred Rampton looked up, his eyes steely. The unhappiness and dissatisfaction of his mouth turned to un-
pleasantness. 'What the hell's that supposed to mean?'

'I merely asked—'

'This Planning Committee—what'll you be saying to
them?'

'I assure you—'

'Lissen, mister, you better watch your mouth when you
get to that Planning Committee. This is big business; it's
not just me who's involved. There's money and more tied
up in this, so if you think you're going to start any little
hares—'

'I think,' Arnold said firmly, 'I'd better be leaving.'

The only demur that Fred Rampton gave to the sug-
gestion was obscenities he did nothing to muffle.

In the flagged corridor James Rampton's personal
uneasiness broke through. He touched Arnold upon the
shoulder; Arnold turned in the dimness and stared at
him. 'You don't want to pay much heed to my uncle,' he
said.

'I don't believe he understands the implications of the
whole thing,' Arnold complained.

'I'll be working on him,' James Rampton said, with an earnestness that brought out the sweat on his upper lip. 'I know how things can go in these planning committees — the old man doesn't know, or doesn't care.'

'I have no influence on such occasions,' Arnold said, a trifle primly.

James Rampton stared at him for a moment and then walked past him, to stand in the yard. He looked about him with distaste. 'I know what you'll be thinking about this place.' He kicked disconsolately at one of the scrawny dogs.

'I don't know that my feelings have much relevance, in the circumstances.'

'I know otherwise. You'll be putting in the report. You got to understand, Mr Landon. This farm, it's been going to ruin for years. I don't really know how it all started, but when the old woman — Uncle Fred's mother — was alive, things ran pretty well. She was a right old bitch,' he added admiringly.

Arnold looked around him. It was difficult to envisage that this farm has ever thrived. But it was possible.

'When she died,' James Rampton continued, 'things changed. Fred never really had his heart in the farm, seems to me. He's a funny old devil; I mean, he's worked this farm for more than thirty years but somehow he's never had the drive to do anything with it. Know what I mean? It's just staggered along, year by year. Gradually going downhill. Maybe if he'd married, if he'd had a woman to push him, tidy him . . . but he didn't, and if he had, anyway, maybe I wouldn't be here now.' James Rampton raised his head as though sniffing at the wind, seeking out reasons and remembrances.

'You have a personal involvement?' Arnold asked.

James Rampton inspected his work-stained boots and his ragged cuffs. 'When Fred dies, this farm will be mine. He's got no other kinfolk. And me, I'm no farmer. Got no real interest. I'd only sell up. So I'm all for Fred's plan, all for the application. I'll inherit Fred's money when he's gone, and if this application goes through there'll be a hell of a lot of money. Lot more than any other way — money for everyone,' he added meaningfully.

Arnold was ruffled. 'I've already explained: I have no influence. And even if I did —'

'Influence?' James Rampton's voice rose querulously. 'If you got no influence, who has? You'll be writing a report —'

'A factual report —'

'And it'll be putting views forward — Fred's views, Ben Kelvin's views, Colonel Summers's views too for all I know. What I'm saying, Mr Landon, is that this application is important to Fred and it's bloody important to me! I want to be away from this sour damned land, and I want that money in the bank. And if I thought you'd be saying anything bad that would be standing in the way of our application —'

'I don't think you'd better go any further, Mr Rampton,' Arnold suggested. 'You have a misconception with regard to my . . . ah . . . function, and you are in danger of saying things you might later regret.'

For a moment, as he watched the blood recede from James Rampton's face, Arnold thought the man was going to lose his temper completely. The moment passed, however. Rampton managed a ragged smile that was completely lacking in pleasure and stood to one side.

'You'll want to be completing your work, Mr Landon. I won't hold you up any longer. But . . .' the smile faded. 'I hope we understand each other.'

Arnold's chest was fluttery. 'I hope *you* understand *me*, Mr Rampton.'

And boldly he strode out across the littered yard.

The interviews with Fred and James Rampton had shaken

him. The rhythm of his work had been disturbed; he found himself unable to concentrate in the way he normally did, following a pattern of activity that enabled him to move sensibly and logically across the ground he had to cover, making his meticulous, ordered notes, adding small sketches as *aides mémoires* on occasion, and quartering the area in accordance with the map that he carried in his mind. Now, disturbed as he was he found that the job took longer than he had anticipated or planned; the rancour of Fred Rampton, the veiled bribery and then threats of James Rampton, had taken their toll of his control, negating the normal patterns he established.

The noon sun broke through briefly but by two in the afternoon the grey clouds had gathered again. There was still an hour's work left for him and when that hour was done he discovered he still had not covered one small area on the eastern boundary. The Senior Planning Officer would not have approved of this haphazard manner of working.

At three o'clock in the leaden, heavy afternoon Arnold finally completed his survey. His head was throbbing and he felt vaguely unwell. He was not accustomed to feeling this way when he was out in the open air; it led to a massive disinclination to return to the office. So he did something he had never done before during his years with the Planning Department. He quite deliberately decided not to return, but to stay out here, doing nothing. It should have rested him. It didn't.

Conscience bothered him. He should have been on the way to Morpeth; there was time to do an hour's work at his desk, on the documents in his case, before returning to the solitude of his bungalow. Staying here in the fields of Rampton Farm, under the heavy, thundery sky, was wrong. Disconsolately, he trudged across the meadow and began to climb the hill.

And something he had almost lost in the years between, until he had come to the Planning Department, was with him now. The thunder was a faraway growl, the skies were lightening, but Arnold remained in the barn, staring about him as the softness and the darkness and the ancient peace of the place reached out to him, caressed him, whispered to him as no woman had ever done.

Above him, the rafters curved away into the darkness, seeming to reach up to the sky, and Arnold wanted to touch those ancient timbers, learn from them the way his father had learned, and taught him.

He found the ladder in the corner; he reached the top of the hayloft, and after that he was climbing across the roof ties and the dust of centuries was in his nostrils. It was warm here, and soft and protective. A shaft of sunlight now broke through and there were the specks of dust, gleaming like shimmering jewels against the blackness of the walls. They picked out the smooth, curving arch of the roof, warmed the living timber, and Arnold reached out to touch the ribs, caress them, listening to his father speak across the years.

And then, once again, almost imperceptibly it changed. It was wrong, the sense of peace was leaving him. The wood under his fingers was old and it was talking to him, telling him something. He smoothed it, caressed it, bent close to it until his eyes were inches from its dark, old surface. But there was something wrong, something out of place. He sought for it, with his fingers and with his mind and with all the stored knowledge of two generations. And when he found the answer he could not believe it.

After a little while Arnold stretched back, lying full length along the broad beam that supported him. He stared at the blackness of the roof above his head and he waited until the singing in his head subsided, until the painful pounding in his chest had died away. Then he leaned up again and touched the wood, stroked it, levered himself forward until he could peer closely at it again and seek the impossibility of a fingernail insertion in the joint.

When he was absolutely certain, he climbed down again, his heart thundering uncontrollably in his chest. The skies outside were blue again, the clouds rolled back like a grey, unwanted carpet, but Arnold did not go outside. Instead, he crouched down in the old barn, leaning against the wall, his head low between his hands, and he began to cry, for his father, for himself, and for all the beauty in the world, his world, his father's world.

It was only hours later, as he was driving across the rolling hills above the Coquet that Arnold Landon suddenly realized he had information that would blow apart the planning application in respect of Rampton Farm.

CHAPTER 2

1

If there was anything the Senior Planning Officer disliked intensely it was unpredictability. He wanted an ordered existence, everything in its place, a pattern of life that left him perfectly clear as to what the morrow would bring. It was one reason why he suffered his wife's cottage pie on Thursdays: the predictability of it suited him even if the culinary consequences were disastrous and the gastric results devastating. But something had gone wrong last night: it was only Tuesday, and his wife had served up cottage pie. As the Senior Planning Officer had rumbled through the dark hours he had felt a sense of desperation: the fabric of his world was unravelling at the edges and panic churned amid his gastric disorders. And now, the following morning, there was the complete documentation on the Rampton Farm planning application. The Senior Planning Officer sighed unhappily.

Arnold had done a good job, as usual. It was true there was a surprising *raggedness* about some of the later notes he had taken, a certain looseness regarding part of the survey, and for once Arnold had seen fit to introduce an irrelevancy into his report: comments concerning the possibility of a buried village on the hill. The Senior Planning Officer had asked Arnold about that.

'Why did you include that, Arnold?' he had asked.

'It's not exactly relevant to the planning proposal,' had come the unsatisfactory reply, 'but in a sense it does underline what I have noted about the Old Wheat Barn.'

The cottage pie could not have finally completed its tour of the Senior Planning Officer's vitals, for his stomach lifted unpleasantly. The Old Wheat Barn. Yes.

'I like a *clean* enquiry,' the Senior Planning Officer said plaintively.

'I know that, sir.'

'This barn thing . . . I don't know, Arnold.' The Senior Planning Officer had not told the truth at that point. He *did* know, really; he had already made up his mind, in a hazy sort of way. He was a professional. So was Arnold. But Arnold was different: the Senior Planning Officer recognized that a man with Arnold's passion for the past, feeling for materials, depth of understanding of things that were beyond the Senior Planning Officer's comprehension, such a man was bound to be different. But professionalism was something else: it demanded that a man use a blue pencil from time to time, in the interest of clean, uncluttered advocacy and the pursuit of truth.

Besides, such . . . statements would lend an air of unpredictability to the Planning Committee deliberations that was certainly unwelcome.

Even so, it was as well to be sure, in advance.

The Senior Planning Officer picked up the telephone and rang the university switchboard. When the pert, middle-class tones of the girl with two upper-firsts and a lower-second lover in the Chemistry Department answered, he said in his best official accent: 'This is the County Senior Planning Officer. May I be connected with Professor John Fisher, if you please?'

Three hours later, after a careful lunch of polystyrene-flavoured slimming biscuits and some watery cottage cheese, the Senior Planning Officer flicked some invisible fluff from his immaculate grey suit, tucked the manila folder under his arm, smiled at Arnold and marched out of his office with Arnold a respectful two paces behind him. He nodded vaguely to several people passing in the corridor and acknowledged two men in the lift. They emerged on the first floor and made their way along to the committee room abutting on to the Council Chamber.

The square-built room gleamed with polished wood and the sunshine streamed in through the tall, bright windows. The leather of the chairs shone green, with the embossed arms picked out brightly on the chairman's seat. The Senior Planning Officer walked along beside the tables, checking that the appropriate agenda papers had been laid in their places; from the corner of his eye he noticed that Arnold, as usual, was running his hands over the wood of the old table at the back of the room—not the modern, highly polished tables along the length of the room but the old ceremonial table that had been thrown out of the Council Chamber and relegated to this room as a depository for unwanted papers. Some day the Senior Planning Officer would ask the Chairman if they should get rid of that table. He could guess where there might be a home for it.

The Senior Planning Officer finally declared himself

satisfied and glanced at his watch. It lacked but ten minutes to the appointed hour: he glanced up, nodded to the doorman and that official marched across the carpeted hall outside to admit those applicants and members of the public who desired admittance.

They came filing in, somewhat subdued by the hushed atmosphere of the committee room and the presence of the two sober-suited officials sitting with their papers in front of them.

From the corner of his mouth, Arnold advised the Senior Planning Officer of the identities of some of those who entered. The Senior Planning Officer appreciated the stage whisper: it was as well to know who was present on these occasions. 'That's Mr Fred Rampton,' Arnold husked. 'And the gentleman taking the seat beside him is his nephew, James Rampton.' After a pause he added, 'And the man who's just come in to sit near the window, that's one of the objectors to the scheme: Mr Kelvin, from Newman Farm.'

But the Senior Planning Officer was no longer listening. Instead, he was concentrating covertly on the heavily built man seated just behind Fred Rampton. Everything about his face seemed to denote determination and strength: it was as though his features had been put together in a string of clichés. His jaw was square, his mouth set in an aggressive line. He had dark yet piercing eyes and his eyebrows formed a thick, strong line above those eyes. His hair was glossy and black, streaked with grey above the ears and his whole attitude was one of dominance and power, from the way he sat, erect and sharp-eyed, to the manner in which his large hands were clasped, rigid-fingered, on the table in front of him, resting on the papers neatly placed in a pile. The Senior Planning Officer had seen him before, had in fact been introduced to him on one junketing occasion. His name was Charles Burke and he was a man to contend with. Or rather, the Senior Planning Officer reconsidered, a man with whom one was not wise to contend. He did not repay Arnold's compliment by pointing out Charles Burke to him.

Nor did he explain to Arnold who the slight man in the blue suit was, slipping into the seat at the end of the row and smiling slightly, nodding to the Senior Planning Officer as he did so.

In a little while, as the seats behind filled up, the members of the Planning Committee began to arrive: little Mrs Oldroyd, determinedly sixty and determinedly first, as always. Peter Fenton, the son of the local butcher in Morpeth arrived next: his ambition to get on in local politics was matched only by his determination to keep out of his father's shops. *That* man, the Senior Planning Officer considered, could well see logic in supporting Charles Burke and Fred Rampton: whizzkids were supposed to be behind thrusting new ideas in business. Fussy Mr Nicholas came in fussily as usual: good-hearted but inevitably having lost his papers. Resignedly, the Senior Planning Officer passed him a spare set from his emergency file, and smiled thinly in return for the effusive thanks. After him came a rash of committee members, presumably having been imbibing together in the members' dining-room. That could sometimes make for a lively meeting, if not a terribly constructive one. Last, and certainly not least, and positively determined to sweep in at the rear where the finest effect could be made, came the chairman, Colonel Summers, white fluffy hair standing up from above his ears, choleric blue eyes already gleaming at prospects of battle, and the usual gaping of his blue-striped shirt to reveal a yellow vest, flashing at his navel. It might have been his ample girth that did it; it might have been his wife's inability as a seamstress. The Senior Planning Officer guessed it was something much more psychologically deep-rooted. For the life of him he could not understand what it might be.

Colonel Summers tapped the table in front of him, the gavel underlining his importance. The meeting was to begin. The Senior Planning Officer waited silently, checking through his file as the Chairman took them all through Apologies, Minutes of the Last Meeting, Matters Arising, and sighed as Mr Nicholas raised once again the accuracy of the wording of two resolutions. Mr Nicholas was a retired solicitor: the Senior Planning Officer wondered how many of his clients' papers he must have lost over the years.

Then, finally, they came to the business of the meeting.

There were three applications to be dealt with: an extension of a bungalow on an estate to the north of Morpeth, an application to convert two houses into a public house, and the Rampton Farm/Brandling Leisure Pursuits application for change of user. The first one was dealt with quickly; the second necessitated some statements from the brewery company representative and the Senior Planning Officer was called upon to express a view. He did so, with appropriate succinctness. 'The papers are not complete, Mr Chairman. I would advise referral back to the next meeting. I will, meanwhile, undertake consultations with the brewery company.' It was agreed.

'And now,' Colonel Summers said, raising his round face and seeming to sniff the wind, 'we have before us the planning application relating to Rampton Farm. I presume one of the applicants will wish to make an initial statement?'

The Senior Planning Officer glanced towards Fred Rampton and Charles Burke but neither moved. Instead, a dark-suited gentleman with a Celtic look about him rose to his feet. His tone was practised and smooth. 'I represent the applicants, Mr Chairman — Mr Farnum of Todd and Mason.'

The Senior Planning Officer grimaced. Brandling Leisure Pursuits would have arranged this—legal representation. He sat up and listened, while the smooth young solicitor outlined the application on behalf of Mr Fred Rampton. It was a good performance. The Senior Planning Officer observed the effect the peroration had upon the members of the committee. As Farnum outlined the argument, stressing that Mr Rampton, in requesting the planning permission, was merely preparing the ground—and Farnum paused to allow his audience to enjoy the pun—for Brandling Leisure Pursuits, who had taken up an option to purchase on the land, to undertake a significant strengthening of the region's tourist industry.

'You will appreciate, lady and gentlemen, that of recent years, with the decline both of the fishing and mining industries in the north-east, and the relative standstill that has occurred in agriculture, it is more than ever necessary to develop new industries. The answer has been obvious, staring us in the face: the region has an unparalleled sweep of coastline, breathtaking grandeur in its hills and forests, and if we can increase the tourist industry by capitalizing upon these assets we introduce new, vigorous blood into the area.'

Like Mr Charles Burke, the Senior Planning Officer thought sourly.

'The area to the west of the county has taken a share of the tourist industry,' Farnum was continuing, 'but has remained largely undeveloped for all that. If Mr Rampton obtains the necessary planning permission, he will enter into an agreement with Brandling Leisure Pursuits to carry out the kind of change of user that is stated in these planning papers. It will result in a new way of life for many people; it will result in employment opportunities; and it will rejuvenate an area which of recent years has gone into decline.'

And when Farnum had completed his statement, it was the turn of the objectors. There were four in all, but it was Ben Kelvin who came across most forcefully, as a successful neighbouring farmer and one most likely to be affected by the change of user. His style was unlike Farnum's but that was no bad thing: he came across as honest and involved. He denied some of the points in Farnum's opening remarks: the area had not gone into decline, for his own farm was witness to that; there were already employment opportunities in the villages, in traditional skills, agriculture and forestry; and the kind of development that was envisaged by Brandling Leisure Pursuits was foreign to the area, foreign to the lifestyle of the inhabitants and destructive of the Northumberland way of life.

The Senior Planning Officer noted that the arguments did little to persuade Peter Fenton on the committee: he leaned back, hardly listening, his mind already made up after the remarks made by Farnum. But the others were still doubtful, and the Senior Planning Officer was aware of the steely glance directed towards Ben Kelvin by the redoubtable Charles Burke: the man could recognize an enemy when he saw one. The Senior Planning Officer sighed. He merely trusted that Mr Kelvin also could pick an enemy out of a crowd.

There was a brief discussion among the committee members in which Fenton seemed to be urging some course of action, probably precipitate, the Senior Planning Officer thought, and which the Chairman was denying, still considerate of the shooting rights of his friends.

Colonel Summers glowered down towards the Senior Planning Officer. 'Is there any advice the officers might wish to give the committee at this stage?'

It was the Senior Planning Officer's moment. He rose to his feet and adjusted his left wrist cuff. 'Thank you, Mr

Chairman. There are a few observations we would wish to make.' He was conscious of Arnold staring up at him, waiting, and he cleared his throat, nervously. He liked enquiries of this kind to be clean, uncluttered.

'Well, carry on,' Colonel Summers said testily.

'We have gone through the planning application very thoroughly, Mr Chairman, and my colleague has also undertaken a complete survey of the farm itself, and the neighbouring area. The detailed remarks regarding the environment are to be found on page three of the documents in front of you, extending to page eight. If I may be permitted . . .'

Painstakingly, the Senior Planning Officer led the committee through the details, before directing their attention to the plans also submitted cartographically.

'We've already read all this,' Colonel Summers grumbled, casting a choleric glance upwards to the ceiling. The cherubs gambolled on, unheeding.

'Quite so, Mr Chairman, but if you will bear with me . . . The result of the general survey would seem to show that there can be no major activities noted in the application to which the committee can take exception *legally*, or in matter of principle . . .' From the corner of his eye the Senior Planning Officer was aware of Charles Burke shifting in his seat, clearly satisfied by the statement. 'On the other hand, it is the duty of the committee to consider the environmental disturbance which will take place and the impact upon the community by the change of user. On these matters, at this stage, the officers would wish to express no opinion.' He sat down, satisfied, but aware that Arnold was not.

'What about the barn?' Arnold whispered.

The Senior Planning Officer frowned, and shook his head.

'But—'

The Senior Planning Officer shook his head again, and

leaned forward to listen to the discussion that had begun among the members. It soon became apparent that there was a division of opinion. The Chairman was far from impartial: he had in mind the woodland above the farm and the shooting rights beyond that would clearly be affected by the development projected. Fenton, on the other hand, was of the opinion that this was a desirable development for the region, as intimated by the case put forward by Farnum, and the young turk had several members of the committee with him. As the Senior Planning Officer listened, he began to suspect it would all come down to which way fussy Mr Nichols and dim Mrs Oldroyd leaned.

And neither of them responded well to pressure — not the kind of pressure that Peter Fenton was placing upon them.

They were still arguing almost an hour later, with occasional contributions from the cool Mr Farnum and the gruff Ben Kelvin. But when it came to a vote the Senior Planning Officer guessed the application would obtain the necessary support. It was also the guess of Colonel Summers, who was getting redder and redder in the face as the time went by. Arnold was shifting unhappily in his seat beside the Senior Planning Officer as Peter Fenton pressed the Chairman for a vote to be taken. Reluctantly, desperately, the Chairman of the Planning Committee cast around for help.

'Are there any more points to be made; any more arguments to be raised?'

The Senior Planning Officer was silent. Arnold was still stirring restlessly in his seat as the Senior Planning Officer collected his papers, and looked across to the blue-suited man at the end of the row. *He* seemed disappointed; the Senior Planning Officer was not.

'Well, if there are no further comments . . .' the Chairman said unhappily, and to the horror of the Senior

Planning Officer Arnold Landon got to his feet.

For one wild moment the Senior Planning Officer almost lost control and dragged Arnold down again. His sense of his position prevented such rash action. Instead, stony-faced to hide his embarrassment, he sat still and stared straight ahead of him.

'There . . . er . . . there is one point the committee should perhaps take into account before reaching a . . . er . . . decision,' Arnold was saying. The blue-suited man at the end of the row leaned forward in obvious interest.

Colonel Summers was relieved, but a little bewildered. He glanced at the Senior Planning Officer uncertainly, but there was no assistance from that quarter. 'Well, Mr . . . er . . .' He hesitated.

'Landon, Mr Chairman. I merely wish to point out that the committee might wish to consider its duties and responsibilities under the Town and Country Planning Regulations of 1972.'

Colonel Summers gaped at him for a moment, then cleared his throat. 'We certainly would, Mr . . . er . . . Landon. But . . . er . . . in precisely what respect?'

'Under the Town and Country Planning Act 1971, Mr Chairman, which was a consolidation of the 1968 provisions, it is an offence to demolish, extend or alter a listed building in any way which would affect its character as a building of special architectural interest unless the work has been authorized by a listed planning consent issued by the local planning authority or the Secretary of State. This is a matter the committee might wish to consider, Mr Chairman.'

Arnold sat down.

The Senior Planning Officer's hands were clammy. This should have been an uncluttered enquiry. But now . . .

Peter Fenton leaned forward to catch the chairman's attention. 'I was not aware that there was any question of listed building consents in this application. The Rampton Farm itself is to be demolished but there is nothing in the papers to suggest the farm has any architectural significance.' He frowned. 'Perhaps Mr Landon could make himself a little more clear.'

At the chairman's nod, Arnold rose again. 'The farm itself, I agree, has no architectural significance. But there is the matter of the barn.'

There was a short silence in the room. Slowly Mr Farnum rose and in his best lawyer's clipped manner announced, 'Mr Chairman, I wish to draw attention to the fact that the barn . . . or any barn . . . on the property is not a listed building.'

'Mr Landon?' the chairman asked warily.

'That is why I made reference to the 1972 Regulations, Mr Chairman. I agree that the old barn is not a listed building. But under the regulations it is open to a planning authority to make application to list a building as one of historical architectural interest.'

'And this barn?'

'I believe the committee should consider its listing.'

A new voice cut across the silence: harsh, forceful, it reverberated in the room. It was Charles Burke's voice.

'What the hell is this all about? Listed buildings? I've never heard that there's any old building on the property that should be listed. It seems to me this is some kind of ploy to delay things. Mr Chairman, why can't we just go ahead and get a decision on this whole thing?' Charles Burke sat back in his chair, angrily, and Peter Fenton was nodding in support.

Colonel Summers was not to be rushed. His blue eyes were alight with the hope that his friends' rough shooting might yet be saved.

'Mr Landon, just why do you consider this building—'

'The Old Wheat Barn,' Arnold supplied.

'The Old Wheat Barn should be made the subject of a

listed building submission?' the Chairman continued.

Arnold raised his head and the Senior Planning Officer lowered his as Arnold said, 'Because the Old Wheat Barn is a thirteenth-century structure, Mr Chairman, and should properly be the subject of a listed building order.'

There was a short silence. A movement across to the Senior Planning Officer's left resulted in the Chairman's attention being drawn to the blue-suited man at the end of the row. The Senior Planning Officer had hoped it would not come to this.

'Mr Chairman . . .' the blue-suited man said.

'You are . . . ?'

'Professor John Fisher.'

There was a buzz of interest. A reporter, half asleep at the back of the room, was suddenly wide awake.

'You have something to add?' Colonel Summers asked warily.

'Only that the gentleman who just spoke is mistaken. The Old Wheat Barn is a structure that dates from the sixteenth century.'

'No,' Arnold said firmly. 'It is a thirteenth-century building.'

'That,' Professor John Fisher said with emphasis, 'is rubbish.'

The Chairman of the Planning Committee sighed with relief; he had the controversy he would have wished for. He tapped the table with his gavel to announce an adjournment and the Senior Planning Officer caressed his burning temples with clammy fingers.

All he had wanted was a clear, uncluttered enquiry.

2

Arnold had never before appeared on television and the prospect terrified him. It was all so unnerving, and so

had a feeling in his bones about the whole thing. He told
Arnold so. For once Arnold was equivocal about his
respect for the Senior Planning Officer's bones. He was
not sure he was doing the right thing, but he *was* sure
about the Old Wheat Barn.

Whatever Professor John Fisher might have to say
about it.

The television studios were tucked away near the Quay-
side in Newcastle in buildings Arnold had expected to be
rather more prepossessing than they were. Similarly, what
little television he had seen — for he did not have one in
the cottage and had merely watched a few programmes,
in the local pub, devoted to the English Heritage — had
led him to expect a certain degree of lavish entertainment
that was not forthcoming. He was sent by the porter at
the door to seek out a certain Miss Fanshaw-White. She
turned out to be a bright, chattery young thing in a tight-
waisted blouse, who seemed to know everyone as 'Darling'
and was desperately keen to provide Arnold with a cup of
tea in a rather dismal canteen, before disappearing with
the promise she'd attend to him in due course. After half
an hour a rather precious gentleman called Rodney
introduced himself and described his function as floor
manager for the programme. Then Arnold was left alone
again for a further twenty minutes.

Until Professor John Fisher arrived.

'Ah. Hello, Landon. Thought I'd find you in here.
Guessed the bastards would drop you with a cup of tea
while they pandered to that fellow Burke.'

'Charles Burke?'

'That's right. It'll be a threesome. Jolly, don't you
think?' He looked carefully at Arnold. 'You *don't* think.'

'I'm not sure I should be here at all,' Arnold remarked
truthfully.

'Well, I'm damned sure *I* should be here. After all, I

more or less engineered it.' Fisher smiled broadly, a slight foxy-faced man with a high opinion of himself. Since the afternoon of the committee meeting, Arnold had taken the trouble to look up Professor John Fisher. The man was a historian with a chair at a northern university and an impressive list of publications about the Middle Ages to his name. But he was also a publicist of note and a man who had spent a considerable amount of time in radio and television work, so that he had made a name for himself in the popular as well as the academic world of architecture and social history. He was used to events such as the *Northern Lights* programme and knew what to expect. Arnold, on the other hand, had no idea what was likely to happen.

'Anyway,' Fisher was saying as he sat down at the dingy table beside Arnold, 'I thought it might be useful if we had a chat about all this, fill in some background before we get into the studio and hammer away with Burke. He's just background fodder, of course—oh, I mean, they're shoving whisky down his throat at the moment and making him think he's no end of an important man—television people have such *small* minds, you know—but it's you and I who will be making the main impact on the programme. So we'd better lay down some ground rules before we start.'

'Ground rules?'

Fisher nodded emphatically. 'I'd better make it clear why I decided to push this whole thing in the first instance. At the University there are certain internal political moves to downgrade the status of mediæval history studies. I've no doubt I can fight a respectable rearguard action, but I happen to *believe* in the importance of such studies and there's the chance of a considerable endowment arising shortly from the Beddowes family. I'd like to make some mileage out of the media during the next few months, and this could well be an important leg-up in the campaign, you see what I mean?'

Arnold didn't, but agreed he did. It seemed simpler, in this bewildering world.

'So,' Fisher continued, 'I don't want the gist of your argument here and now, because that would take some of the freshness out of the debate when it hots up. And I'll try to make it hot, even though you're clearly wrong—'

'But I'm not,' Arnold said.

Fisher was slightly taken aback. His pale blue eyes filmed over in vague disbelief, and then he brushed the film and the doubt away with a wave of his hand. 'Yes, well, stick to that and we can battle it out. But remember, much of my *drive* will be manufactured, so don't get upset, don't lose your cool, and don't lose the thread of your argument. There has to be a certain *balance*, or else you'll be seen clearly as the underdog and audience sympathy could well lean away from academic judgment to emotion. We want *both*, but in the end . . . What's the matter, Mr Landon?'

Arnold shook his head muzzily. 'I don't really have much idea what you're talking about, Professor.'

Fisher regarded him blankly. 'You *are* going to maintain that the Old Wheat Barn is thirteenth-century?'

'I am.'

Fisher nodded, breathing a sigh of relief. 'Well, that's all right, then. I mean if you didn't, there'd be no theory for me to demolish, would there?' He paused for a moment, gazed at Arnold thoughtfully, and then dismissed the thought with a brief smile. He reached for his silver cigar case and lit up again. 'Where did you take your degree, Landon?'

'Degree?'

Fished seemed vaguely baffled. He drew on his cigar, waved it negligently. 'Was it History . . . Social Studies . . . or was it Town Planning?'

'I think you misunderstand, Professor,' Arnold said slowly.

'I have no background in any of those things. And I have no—'

'No degree,' Professor Fisher said. 'Bloody hell.' He contemplated the end of his glowing cigar. 'I'm sorry, old man. Didn't mean to sound . . . ah . . . patronizing. So . . . er . . . what is your background, then?'

'Background?'

'Education,' Fisher said a trifle impatiently. 'Experience.'

'I'm afraid,' Arnold said, 'you would regard my education as somewhat . . . rudimentary.'

'Try me,' Fisher said, but there was a note of caution in his voice.

'Secondary school. No examination successes to talk about, except woodwork, metalwork, technical drawing. Then, the Town Clerk's Department.'

'As . . . ?'

'A conveyancing clerk.'

Fisher puffed on his cigar. He seemed suddenly nervous. 'And then?'

'After eight years I moved into the Planning Department.'

'Professional qualifications? Surveying? Chartered—'

Arnold took a deep breath. 'I'm afraid, Professor Fisher, I've never taken a professional examination in my life.' And when he heard the soft groan emanating from the don's chest, Arnold felt sorry that he had never subjected himself to such immolation.

'Now let's get this straight,' Fisher said after a short silence. 'You have no education beyond . . . sixteen. You have no professional qualifications. So I suppose you would—' A faint, hopeful expression crossed his narrow features—'I suppose you have a deep and passionate interest in local history?'

'I'm afraid not. Just wood.'

'*Wood*!' Professor Fisher was not only baffled, he was angry. 'Look here, Landon, are you trying to make a fool out of me? When the Senior Planning Officer passed that hypothesis across to me and asked my opinion I was prepared to devote *time* to it because I took it seriously, and was inclined to accept it was the result of serious research and enquiry in the Planning Department. It was arrant nonsense, of course, but even so I set aside time to *look* at it. And I was interested enough to attend the planning meeting to discover the arguments. They weren't forthcoming, so I saw it as a splendid opportunity to get some media mileage, and have the debate thrashed out before a large audience. Academic and popular appeal, that's what I said to the producer of *Northern Lights*. And he took my word for it, because he trusts me. *Trusts*, Landon! I use the media, and I have a reputation with it, one that I'm jealous to protect. I know I'm sneered at by some of my colleagues for the exposure I get on the box, but I know what I'm doing—and I'm good at it. I'm selling my subject, and I'm getting financial support for the university department! And now you tell me I've been conned into having a stand-up debate with someone who's got no background and . . . and whose passion is . . . *wood*?'

The chattery Miss Fanshaw-White and the precious Rodney were standing in the doorway of the canteen, beckoning to them. Behind them stood the heavily-built form of Charles Burke. There was a grimness about the set of his mouth that suggested to Arnold that he was looking forward to the interviews no more than Arnold was—not for the same reasons maybe, but unlike Arnold, and more in tune with Professor Fisher's objectives, he would be out to use the programme as a platform.

Professor Fisher was still staring at Arnold, the burning cigar unheeded in his fingers. 'This isn't going to work,' he muttered, and then he caught sight of Miss Fanshaw-White and Rodney in the doorway, and he groaned. 'Bloody hell. Too late now. All right, old chap, do the best you can. Try for God's sake to keep your end up . . . and if you dry up I'll try to maintain a modicum of interest for the viewers in the whole damned fiasco!'

3

The red light came on and Miss Fanshaw-White straightened in her chair, tightened the blouse over her breasts by the simple expedient of breathing in and pulling in her tummy and smiled at the winking cameraman. 'Good evening, and welcome,' she said breathily. 'And this is *Northern Lights.*' She smiled. Toothily.

Rodney was making waving motions with his limp-wristed hands. Miss Fanshaw-White waited until the background music had faded and then she began.

'We have in the studio this evening three people who are locked in battle over what some might regard as an esoteric discussion but which to one of them, at least, is an important, non-academic matter. Mr Charles Burke, if I may speak to you first, what is your interest in the matter which is engaging public attention—the age of the Old Wheat Barn?'

Burke might have displayed impatience both at the planning committee and while waiting for the programme to start, but he now gave a good account of himself, succinctly, forcefully and positively. He explained that he was involved as a director of Brandling Leisure Pursuits; that the scheme as a whole would bring numerous benefits to the western part of the region; and that while he had every sympathy with the conservationists, he was nevertheless of the opinion that progress was necessary, that jobs were necessary, and that a changing way of life was essential. And that meant a change in attitudes, too.

'I presume,' Miss Fanshaw-White said sweetly, hitching at the hem of her skirt as she swivelled in her chair, 'that cuts right across your views, Professor Fisher.'

'Not entirely,' the Professor said, well versed in the system.

Smoothly, Miss Fanshaw-White went on. 'Professor John Fisher, our second guest this evening, it well known to many viewers. In the academic world he is noted for his work on manorial tithes and mediæval church architecture, for his best-selling works on *Northumberland Manorial Rolls* and *Rambles in Coquetdale*, but he has also made a reputation as a raconteur, local commentator and panel game chairman. What particular guise do you wear this evening, John?'

Professor Fisher smiled. 'Well, Virginia, a mixture of both, I suppose—that is, academic and debater. You see, while I would agree with much of what Mr Burke has to say, I cannot, as an historian, go along with him all the way. There are things we must preserve . . .'

Arnold felt hot. As Professor Fisher continued to elaborate about all that was worthwhile in the heritage of the past and about the need to balance it against the demands of the future Arnold found himself beginning to sweat under the hot lights. He simply did not understand what he was doing here. He knew what he knew, but he suspected that in the falseness, the spuriousness of this atmosphere, he would never have the opportunity to explain what he knew and believed in.

'So,' Virginia Fanshaw-White announced, laughing merrily, 'with *that* comment I'll turn to our third guest of the evening, Mr . . . er . . . Mr Arnold Landon. As many viewers may be aware, Mr Landon is concerned as an officer connected with the planning enquiry and while he is not speaking with authority of the council on these matters, we believe he does have a personal point of view to make. What do you say to that, Mr Landon?'

'Um,' Arnold said.

Virginia Fanshaw-White smiled benignly. 'You did have something controversial to say at the planning enquiry.'

'Ah.'

'And the local press reported,' Miss Fanshaw-White continued, her smile freezing at the edges, 'that you held these views sincerely.'

There was a short silence. It was broken by Professor Fisher. Leaning forward casually, white-knuckled with sudden tension, he said, 'Yes, Mr Landon had a disputable theory about the age of the Old Wheat Barn, located on the Rampton property, and the possible subject of a listed building protection order—which would seriously affect the planning application—if his theory is correct. It is, of course, wrong.'

'Glug,' Arnold offered.

'I have made a study of the area in the past,' Fisher said smoothly, 'and five years ago I actually produced a paper on the Old Wheat Barn. I made a close study of the manorial rolls, the leases, the parish documents, and was able to show without any shadow of doubt that the building, though old, is certainly not as old as Mr Landon suggests. In fact, I can categorically state that the earliest reference to it is found in a tithe payment dated 1541. So it would follow from that—'

'1349,' Arnold said distinctly, and Miss Fanshaw-White swooped like a relieved and hungry hawk.

'Precision, Mr Landon,' she cooed. 'How can you *be* so precise?'

'Secret nocked lap joint,' Arnold said, and inside him he felt the power grow.

'*Secret . . . nocked . . . lap . . . joint,*' Miss Fanshaw-White said in uncomprehending stupefaction. A brief silence fell. Professor Fisher was the first to recover.

'You said 1349. So it isn't thirteenth century you claim, after all! It's fourteenth!'

'Yes,' Arnold agreed. 'I'm sorry. A slip of the tongue.'

Professor Fisher smiled bleakly now that Arnold had found words. 'In the academic life, and dealing with facts of history, one cannot afford to have slips of the tongue. But as I was saying, your claim is nonsense. A study of the manorial rolls . . .'

'But that's where mistakes are made. You go about things the wrong way.'

'The wrong way?' Astonishment reverberated in Professor Fisher's tones, but the power was still growing in Arnold, the assurance, the knowledge that what he was saying was right. 'The wrong way,' he insisted. 'I know, I'm fully aware that the historian works from documents and there are plenty around. The archives yield a vast array: leases, deeds, surveys, tax returns, there's a wealth of original documentation, and the experts use it to date buildings. Disputes between landlords, court rolls, church tithings . . . I know all about that, Professor Fisher.'

'And it's the *wrong* way?' Fisher repeated, slightly stunned.

Arnold nodded. 'Of course. A document tells you very little about a building — more about the times, and the people, really. But it's the building itself which is important. The building provides its own documentation — and it's more accurate than pieces of paper which might have been written years after the event. It's what lawyers would call, I believe, original evidence.'

Professor Fisher was recovering. He leaned back in his chair, relaxing. He spread his hands wide, expressively. 'Well, of course, you're saying nothing that's new. We take that into account too. But along with the documentation. And I've already proved conclusively that the Old Wheat Barn is sixteenth-century in its dating.'

'You're wrong.'

This was better. Both Fisher and Virginia Fanshaw-White smiled. The debate was launched. 'And it's this . . . *joint* which is your basis for argument?' she asked sweetly, flicking an amused look towards Fisher.

'That's right. It was the speciality of a man called John of Wetherby.'

'John,' she said. 'Of Wetherby. Er . . . who was he?'

'A carpenter.'

There was a short silence. Fisher cleared his throat. 'I imagine you're implying that this . . . carpenter worked at the Old Wheat Barn?'

'That's right,' Arnold said eagerly. 'And that's how I can be so precise. You see, John of Wetherby's life is well documented. He was born in Yorkshire but moved north when he was about sixteen, probably after completing an apprenticeship. Most of his finest work was done in the Yorkshire abbeys, however, because he moved back there in 1350, after his marriage in Hexham Church that year. He died in 1370. Now I suppose there's the vague possibility he might have come back north to work on the barn after 1350 but it's highly unlikely since by that time he was working on much grander structures. So at the latest I'd settle for 1349, just before his marriage and return to Yorkshire.'

'So, you would?' Professor Fisher leaned forward wolfishly. 'Are you seriously suggesting that you derive all this . . . proof from the discovery of some joint or other in that barn?'

Arnold nodded vigorously. 'I'd better explain. If you knew about wood, if you knew about the way it's shaped, the way it's used by carpenters, you'd understand.'

'I would?' Fisher said sarcastically, raising an eyebrow to the amused Fanshaw-White, who covertly consulted her watch.

'Yes. You'd begin to understand about all the methods the old carpenters used in assembling their buildings.

You'd get to know about the joints that were devised by the master carpenters down the ages. They follow a strict historical sequence, you see, a sequence that you can date as precisely as, well, pottery, for example.'

Fisher thought he detected a flaw in Arnold's thesis. 'Ah, but before we can make assumptions about such sequences, do we not need to investigate their repetitive possibilities?'

'Yes, Mr Landon,' Miss Fanshaw-White said. 'What about the . . . er . . . repetitive possibilities?'

Arnold scratched his long prow of a nose enthusiastically.

'Ah, now then, I must explain. The record of the carpenters does not demonstrate a steady progress towards perfection through the centuries. The history of each particular kind of joint begins in a primitive simplicity. Ingenuity then develops that joint, it reaches a state of perfection . . . and then declines.'

'It falls out of favour?' Fisher asked, interested in spite of himself.

'Something like that. And the separate histories of these individual joints, they do not necessarily coincide in time. In any one building a certain kind of joint may have reached its pitch of perfection while another, invented earlier, might already have become degenerate.'

'Degenerate,' Miss Fanshaw-White breathed. 'Fascinating.' She glanced at the studio clock and then at the producer. He ignored her.

'But what are you saying,' Fisher pressed, 'only demonstrates the essential weakness of your system of dating a building. If these joints do not coincide, and if you accept as you seem to, that craftsmen copy each other's work, how can you possibly suggest a particular joint is the work of one man?'

A harsh voice cut across them. 'You'll forgive me, I'm sure, but my interests are real, rather than academic.

Does this essentially have anything to do with the real facts at issue?' Charles Burke scowled at the camera. 'I'm a businessman. I've no interest in this historical claptrap.'

Miss Fanshaw-White giggled. Things were warming up. Time was running short, but if she could just encourage Mr Burke—'You see your own problems, Mr Burke, as transcending the interests of historical research?'

Burke's heavy eyebrows drew together and he glowered at her. 'I'm concerned only with getting something built—not trying to find out how old something that's already built may be. I've seen this barn. It hasn't been used in years. It'll be in the way of the development I propose. It will have to come down. And discussions such as this get us nowhere. They simply lead to delay in the approval of the planning application.'

'The Philistines are truly among us,' Fisher murmured.

Burke flashed an angry glance at the Professor. 'Weak-kneed parasites like you are only too happy to lean on the Philistines for hard cash when they want support for their ivory-tower schemes!'

Fisher's mouth whitened, and for a moment he almost lost his temper. Then he remembered his television *persona* and his aims and he smiled stiffly. 'That's a point of view we might debate elsewhere, Mr Burke. But Mr Landon hasn't answered my challenge. How can you be sure that a particular joint is the work of one man?'

Arnold considered for a moment, and Miss Fanshaw-White glanced nervously towards the producer. Any moment now he'd be raising his hand in a throat-cutting gesture. 'I think what you fail to take into account,' Arnold said, 'is the pride of craftsmanship. The mediæval master carpenters were the admired, revered artists of their day. They had a long apprenticeship, they developed skills and ingenuity, they possessed inventive powers . . . and, inevitably, vanity. You'll understand . . .

they would not be prepared to keep copying someone else's developed joint; they would each want to introduce variations, the stamp of originality, the mark of a master. But, naturally, there are levels of perfection and once a joint became perfect, later variations, ingenious though they might be, would become, mechanically speaking, far less efficient.'

'I can accept that,' Fisher said, just as Miss Fanshaw-White was about to break in. 'But where does that lead your argument?' He shook his head. 'You're talking of complex matters. Very complex dating matters.'

'Not so complex if you know your materials.'

'But the Old Wheat Barn—'

'Contains an example of a secret nocked lap joint that was used by only one man—John of Wetherby. It was developed during the later part of the thirteenth century but it was this man who brought it to perfection.'

'But others will have used it,' Fisher suggested.

'No, not really. After the early years of the fourteenth century economic conditions were such that speed became important . . . speed and cost. John of Wetherby developed this particular joint and perfected it, but when he was using it the lap joint was already in decline. It was too expensive to use, expensive both in materials and in time. Something cheaper, simpler . . . and worse was soon discovered, and used.' Arnold hesitated, glanced at Miss Fanshaw-White. 'May I show an example?'

Flustered, she looked across to Rodney but the floor manager seemed to have forgotten the time. They were already adrift on timing but he was making no attempt to wind things up. As she raised here eyebrows at him he shook his head fiercely. Unlike Victoria, Rodney knew good television when he saw it.

Arnold drew from his pocket a small piece of smooth, polished wood. Automatically his fingers caressed it as he held it and the zoom lens picked up the touch, transmitted its affection into a thousand homes. 'A lap joint,' Arnold said quietly, 'works like this. The lap joint developed by John of Wetherby was of a particular kind, used for joining two shorter lengths of timber to make one long piece. His joints made it virtually impossible to separate the two lengths, while at the same time the joint resisted those forces to which roofs were subjected — sagging and twisting. You see how it works . . . ?'

Fisher leaned forward. 'But I didn't see . . .'

The camera lens zoomed in as Arnold demonstrated once more. The wood came apart under his fingers, and was locked again.

'Good Lord,' Professor Fisher said. 'I don't think I've ever seen so sophisticated a mechanism. You . . . *you* made that joint?'

Arnold smiled modestly. 'It's a copy of one of John of Wetherby's. His were much larger, of course: this is a tiny replica. But this is his secret nocked lap joint. He, like other carpenters in those days, used green wood for the joints, so that natural shrinkage would force the parts so tightly together that it would be difficult even to see the joint, let alone spring it.'

Miss Fanshaw-White shuffled in her chair. She glanced at Charles Burke. His brow was thunderous. 'I think at this stage —' she began.

'One moment,' Fisher interrupted, coming out of his momentary reverie. 'What you've just said is important. You claim to have found one of these joints in the Old Wheat Barn, and that it proves John of Wetherby had a hand in its building, and ergo, the barn was built around about 1349.'

'That's correct.'

Fisher's eyes flashed triumphantly. 'A fascinating story, Mr Landon, but hardly credible. I'll stick with my documents and similar proofs. That joint there in your hand is hardly to be seen — except by the man who made it: you.

told him and made him believe and love, look, search, feel. Arnold knew that he would have located that joint of John of Wetherby in a blackness deep as pitch — but it was not something that he could have adequately explained to Fisher. It could not depend upon proofs — it required an act of faith.

For a while, after lunch, Arnold toyed with the idea of taking a long walk above Whinsill, on the Roman Wall, but the prospect did not appeal. He could go to Ogle Church, for there were some investigations he wanted to undertake there in his spare time, but he understood there was to be a wedding held there that afternoon. And in any case, his thoughts kept drifting back to the Old Wheat Barn.

Ben Kelvin. He had told Arnold that if he wished to call at Newman Farm to take a look at the sixteenth-century section of the farmhouse he would be welcome at any time. If he went out this afternoon, he might be able to look again in the Old Wheat Barn — but if Fred Rampton denied him access there was still the Newman Farm . . .

Arnold picked up the phone. It was a woman who answered. Mrs Kelvin. No, her husband was across at Hexham that afternoon but she knew about Mr Landon, and if he'd care to call he would be more than welcome. She'd love to have a professional opinion about the old section of the farmhouse. It had been in her family for generations.

Arnold said he would call at the farm about three that afternoon.

The sky was flat and grey, but the hint of sunshine behind the cloud gave the air a strange luminosity that made Arnold squint as he drove along the quiet roads that lifted over the hills towards the western county boundary. He wound down the window and let the cool air play against his face, and there was the scent of woodsmoke in his nostrils, and new-cut grass. Up here, high above the river which gleamed dully in the hazy light, he was a long way distant from the rush of modern life, and more in tune with that part of him that was real—the yearning for the past, the feel for the old world, the understanding and appreciation of the old skills. Perhaps that was what Northumberland meant for Arnold, in essence: the opportunity to lose himself in the years lost to everyone else he knew. He was a man out of his time, but his time was now and he had to accept that. Yet there were still the ancient beauties of the folding hills, the slow-moving rivers, the flash of gorse and heather, and the cackling laughter of the black grouse among the rocks.

He drove on almost in a dream, thinking of the old lost world and then he was brought up against reality as he drew near to Newman Farm: a tractor, trundling along the lane as it had trundled the first time he had come to Rampton Farm. And when the driver of the tractor looked back Arnold realized it was Jack Sorrell.

He was forced to exercise patience as the tractor moved slowly along the narrow lane—there were no places where he could overtake. He was still about a mile from the Newman Farm when Sorrell swung to the left, to make an entry into the field. He cut the tractor engine and got down, still blocking the lane, then walked back towards Arnold.

'You'll have to wait a bit,' he said. 'I got to open the gate and it takes a bit of manoeuvring to get the tractor in.' His dissatisfied eyes widened slightly then, as he recognized Arnold. 'Ah . . . Mr Landon, isn't it?'

'That's right. We met the other day, when you and Mr Kelvin gave me a lift.'

'Right. Saw you last night I did, though. At the George Inn. On telly.' Sorrell's saturnine features were thoughtful. 'Bit of an argument, was there, at the end?'

'How do you mean?'

'That Professor chap. And Mr Burke—him that's pushing this planning application.'

Arnold hesitated. There had been an altercation but he had taken no part in it. As he was leaving he had become aware of Virginia Fanshaw-White's attempts to make the peace between two irate men: Fisher beside himself at the remark from Burke about 'academic poofs' and Burke's frustration at the way the programme had gone, with his views being almost entirely ignored, spilling over into anger. When Arnold had left, Burke had been half-lifting the smaller Professor Fisher off his feet, by the lapels. It seemed as though he had not entirely set aside his physically-orientated origins. 'Well, yes, I think there was a bit of a squabble,' Arnold agreed.

'Thought so.' Sorrell's eyes were flecked with green; somehow, it seemed to emphasize the dissatisfaction that touched the man's whole bearing like a cancerous growth. 'Doesn't do to tangle with a man like that Burke feller. Dangerous. Lost his temper there, in the open; from what I hear it's worse when he don't—things can happen behind the scenes, like.'

Arnold guessed Sorrell was talking about Burke's supposed involvement in the Scotswood murder.

'Mind you,' Sorrell was continuing, half to himself, 'they make a right pair, that Burke chap and old Fred Rampton. Right pair of bastards, if you ask me.'

Arnold glanced at the man curiously. 'You used to have a farm around here at one time, didn't you?'

The green-flecked eyes held his for a long, dissatisfied moment. 'That's right, Mr Landon. Just over the hill there, beyond the woods. Nice little place; good land. But it had one problem: water rights. It drained too well, and I had to have a source for the couple of cattle I kept. Rampton wouldn't co-operate, wouldn't let me pipe in. And then there was trouble over fencing. Took me to law, he did, the old bastard. Cleaned me out. I had to sell up. That's when I started working for Mr Kelvin.'

'I'm sorry.'

Anger stirred in the green-flecked eyes, an old anger, slow but deep-seated and dangerous. 'Sorry? Aye. Well, there's one who'll be a damn sight sorrier, one day, mark my words.' A moment later it was apparent he wished the words had not been blurted out, let alone marked. Sorrell turned away, bad-temperedly. 'I'll get this gate open.'

Ten minutes later Arnold drove down the track to Newman Farm. Mrs Kelvin was already waiting for him when he entered the yard.

She was a tall woman, but now bowed somewhat by arthritis. She was standing in the doorway, leaning on a stick and when she smiled in welcome the smile softened the lean angularity of her face. Her features were plain, and he suspected that as a girl she would have been rawboned and ungainly, but her eyes were a warm brown, friendly, and though her voice had a harsh timbre her words were welcoming, as she led the way inside the farmhouse.

'I saw you last evening on the television,' she said. 'It was quite a performance, Mr Landon. You were very good. The programme was far too short for my taste. I could have listened to you for much longer.'

The telephone shrilled at the back of the house and Mrs Kelvin looked at him in alarm. 'Oh, dear, I'd better answer that. I'm always worried when Ben's away, I'm afraid something might have happened to him. But you go ahead — if you walk through the kitchen and turn left you'll come up against the section Ben told you about and you said you'd like to see. I'll join you in a little while.'

Alison Kelvin lurched away on her stick, grey head bobbing, and as the telephone shrilled insistently Arnold followed her directions, walked through the broad kitchen, turned left past the pantry and found himself in a narrow storeroom, which, he imagined, would once have played quite a different role in the farmhouse.

The stone copings were obviously old, dressed stone which still bore the marks of adzes, cut in angular nicks that he had seen before. Stone was not Arnold's speciality but this work was familiar to him, and he could roughly date it, in spite of plastering and pointing that had been undertaken upon it for some time. He crouched down, running his hands over the warm stone, and then he inspected the window-ledges, and the old blackened timber that had been used in the construction of the windows themselves.

Fully an hour had passed before he heard the tapping of Alison Kelvin's stick along the stone-flagged passageway but Arnold had been unaware of the passage of time, absorbed as he had been in his inspection.

'I'm sorry I've been so long . . . Ben will be back in an hour or so. You've had time to have a good look around?'

'I have indeed.' Arnold spent the next twenty minutes describing to Alison Kelvin how the original farmhouse had been constructed and the techniques that had been used to build it. He pointed out to her how the stone had been dressed and he advised her that the wood in the timber frames was probably sixty years old. She was a good listener, and there was an intelligent animation in her face as she asked him questions. He found it pleasant talking to someone who displayed an overt interest in her surroundings as she did.

'I've enjoyed this afternoon, and I'm grateful for having the opportunity to take a look around, Mrs Kelvin,' Arnold said at last. 'But I really should not take up more of your time.'

'Nonsense,' she said firmly. 'You must stay to tea. Kitty will be bringing in something to eat shortly and Ben won't be back for a while so you must keep me company. It isn't often we have visitors to Newman Farm.'

Arnold allowed himself to be persuaded.

They walked into the living-room at the back of the house and Arnold gazed around him in surprise. There was a mellowness about the room which he liked, a warm, friendly homeliness emphasized by the depth and comfort of the old furniture. The walls were adorned with paintings, mainly of scenes from the environs of Newman Farm itself, and Mrs Kelvin admitted that they had been done by her when she was a young, single woman.

And standing in the corner of the room was an old harpsichord. Arnold went over to it in admiration.

'Do you play the harpsichord, Mr Landon?'

'No, not at all. But . . . it's beautiful.'

Alison Kelvin came over to stand beside him; she was taller than he was and she leaned past him, ran her fingers over the keys. 'It was built by my grandfather.'

'He was a real craftsman,' Arnold said, and ran his fingers over the stained walnut almost reverently.

'I used to play, long ago. This room used to echo to Bach and Vivaldi. My father . . . but that is all so long ago. Sit down, Mr Landon . . . here's the tea.'

When Kitty had gone Alison Kelvin poured the tea and began to talk about her grandfather, about the harpsichord, about her childhood when the family had been about her and they had had musical evenings in the dark winter months.

'But then it all changed, quite suddenly,' she added sadly. 'It was the war, you understand.'

'What happened?'

'My two brothers. Both were killed. It meant there was no one, except me, to carry on Newman Farm.' She smiled at him, a flickering smile with a hint of long-forgotten wickedness. 'It's strange how things work out in the end, when all is said and done.'

Arnold sipped at his tea. 'How do you mean?'

'Oh, the way things seem, the way they are . . . and the way things then suddenly change. You see, Mr Landon, I was a very unprepossessing child—no, I'm too old for flattery, believe me—and I grew into an ungainly, un-attractive woman. I had one asset, and that only when my brothers died. This farm. And then Ben came along. Strange how things work out.'

'He's done very well at this farm.'

'Oh yes. He's worked hard. He's been a good hus-band . . . Still, tell me about the planning application. Do you think it will go through now?'

'I can't say, Mrs Kelvin.'

'They'll surely make the Old Wheat Barn a listed building after what you said on television last night!'

'I don't believe that follows,' Arnold demurred. 'I wasn't very convincing.'

'You convinced me!' Her old eyes flashed surprisingly. 'And if the truth be known, you half-convinced that Professor Fisher.'

'I don't know. I'm not so sure. Anyway, it'll be up to the committee when they meet next week.'

'Hmmm.' Alison Kelvin leaned back in her chair and stared out of the window to the rise of the hill, the clump of trees at its head, and the half-hidden roof of the Old Wheat Barn. 'Strange . . . until now, I've never liked that old barn. Hearing you talking about it changed things for me—your talk of the old ghosts that inhabit it have exorcized some of mine, I suppose.'

'Ghosts?'

Alison Kelvin laughed, a tinkling sound that was sur-prising in her scrawny throat. 'Oh, we all have ghosts, don't you agree, Mr Landon?' She observed him steadily for a moment, then she smiled. 'Mine was another woman, a woman I never met, but one I've never been quite able to forget.'

'I don't understand, Mrs Kelvin.'

'No, probably not.' She was silent for a little while, gazing out across the hill to the roof of the barn. Then, quietly, she said, 'You'll have realized I am older than my husband, Mr Landon. Seven years, in fact. And I had little to commend me, physically, when we were married. So I had no illusions then; I have none now, though I have certain . . . satisfactions. Because it worked out; Ben's been a good husband, and a good farmer. So I have no complaints. Except the general one about life, I suppose. The fact he never loved me.' Her eyes remain fixed on the hill.

Arnold was embarrassed. He put down his empty cup. 'I'm sure that hasn't been the case—'

She smiled, looked at him and shook her head. 'Have you ever been married, Mr Landon?'

He shook his head.

'The fact is one I faced then, and have always faced,' Alison Kelvin continued. 'Ben married me for the farm, nothing else. I knew it, and I took him on that understanding, even though it was never explicit. Because I loved him. But Ben—'

'You can't really be certain of that—'

'Oh, but I am. You see, he was in love with someone else.' She laughed again. 'This is really rather ridiculous, isn't it, talking about things that happened forty years ago! But I've never talked to anyone about it before, and catharsis is good for the soul, isn't that so? You see, it might all be a long time ago, but the echoes of those days are still reverberating around these hills.'

'How do you mean?'

'Fred Rampton and Ben . . . it's why they have never got on. It was all because of that girl.'

A forty-year-old feud, that was surfacing at last in a planning enquiry, coming out into the open, being exposed but under the cover of something else. In spite of himself, Arnold asked, 'What happened?'

Alison Kelvin sighed and smoothed back an errant wisp of grey hair from her brow. 'Such a long time ago . . . Fred Rampton was living with his mother then. Old Mother Rampton . . . I'm as old now as she was then! She was a strong character, with decided views of life, and she ruled Fred, kept him tied. Until Molly Stavely came to work at Rampton Farm.'

'She's the girl you've been talking about?'

Alison Kelvin nodded. 'That's right. She was a Land Girl—she'd come from Coventry, I think, to work on the land during the early years of the war. I suppose she'd be about nineteen. She stayed just a few months the first time and Fred must have taken a shine to her then. Anyway, she went back home and there was no sign of her for about two years. Then back she came again. By that time Ben was working at Rampton Farm, and my two brothers had just been killed.'

The memory affected her; there was a shine in her eyes as she remembered. Then she shook her head. 'Anyway, I was almost twenty-seven then, all but alone, and I knew Ben, admired him . . . And down at Rampton Farm it seems there was trouble brewing. Fred was keen on Molly Stavely, courting her every chance he got, but never openly under his mother's eye. As for Molly, it seems she played up to him a bit, but she was really more interested in Ben. It began to cause bad blood between them, particularly when they fell to fighting in the yard one day. It seems Old Mother Rampton took a broom handle to the lads and gave them a good hiding. But of course it then came out what they were fighting about.' Alison smiled. 'And that's when the old lady laid the law down. No son of hers was going to be caught by some townee who was all airs and graces. Fred was made to toe the line, and Molly Stavely was sent packing. And in some odd way Fred Rampton blamed Ben. But in fact it wasn't Ben's fault at all. He'd already taken another decision.'

'To marry you?'

Alison looked at him with sober, wise eyes. 'To marry me—or at least, to marry Newman Farm. You see, Mr Landon, it was I who proposed to Ben. I asked him to call, I took him over the farm, I told him that he was a mere labourer at Rampton Farm and I was alone, I needed a husband. With me he would get Newman Farm. Without me, what would he have? And I wanted him.'

Arnold was silent. He wondered about Alison Newman all those years ago. It would take courage to tell a man that she wanted him and was prepared to take the risk of buying him with her possessions.

'I wasn't proud, Mr Landon, and when he came over the following week to tell me he was prepared to wed I might have cried a little but I didn't demand too much of him. He never said he loved me; I never asked him. But we've had a good life and I don't think either of us have had any regrets. At least . . .' She fell silent for a little while.

The harpsichord gleamed warmly in the corner and her eyes drifted to it and there was a hint of sadness in her smile. 'No, no regrets on my part, but as far as Ben was concerned . . . I can't be sure. There were the mornings of those early years, I used to wake and he'd be standing at the window, looking out over the fields. It happened from time to time, he would be lost in a reverie, gazing out there as though he was looking for something he'd lost.' Her glance moved to Arnold. 'He was looking at that old barn up there. It's why, till now, I've never liked it. It was up there they used to meet, you see, Ben and Molly Stavely. It's where they did their courting. But all that, it's long gone now,' and she made a gesture with her hand as though to erase the memory.

'What—' Arnold hesitated—'what happened to Molly Stavely?'

Alison frowned, and shook her head. 'I'm not sure.

Things got a bit unpleasant after that. I don't quite know what happened. I think Ben told her he was getting married to me. There was a row and somehow Mrs Rampton got involved in it. I think she considered Molly a scarlet woman. Anyway, within the week Molly was given her marching orders and away she went, back to Coventry, I suppose. The following month Ben and I were wed. And that was that.'

'One would have supposed that the years between would have healed the breach between Mr Kelvin and Fred Rampton,' Arnold suggested.

'I suppose so. But it didn't happen.' Alison frowned. 'I used to feel sorry for Fred. I think he really loved that girl. His mother dominated him, that was the trouble. But a year or so later Old Mother Rampton died, and Fred was left to run the farm. He left for about six weeks, almost immediately. Talk was he'd gone to Coventry, looking for Molly Stavely, and he went again, for a couple of weeks the following year. But he never found her.'

'Didn't he have her address?'

'The war years. A Land Girl. People drifted. Got killed. No, he never found her. And I think that was the problem. With Fred, the whole thing began to fester. Maybe, if he had got married, had a son, things would have been different. But he didn't: he just brooded about Molly Stavely, became unhappy and introverted, and then as the years went by he saw Ben doing so well with the Newman Farm while his own became sour and neglected . . . his fault, certainly, but maybe he's never seen it that way. Maybe something went out of his life when Molly Stavely went away. Or am I just being a romantic old woman?'

Arnold suspected she was very near the truth about Fred Rampton. He could understand how the man had been soured, and he could understand the bitterness that might lie in Fred Rampton's soul at the thought that Ben

Kelvin might be out to thwart him again, as he had done almost forty years ago.

'It's strange, nevertheless, that Mr Rampton never managed to trace her.'

'They were violent and frantic days, during the war. But it's true . . . once she stepped out of Mrs Rampton's farmhouse that evening no one around here ever heard from her again.'

And it had been left to Fred Rampton to nurse his grudge against Ben Kelvin, and for Ben Kelvin to look out across the fields to the old barn and wonder, perhaps, how things might have been if he had taken a different road.

2

The Planning Committee reconvened the following Tuesday evening. They turned up in full strength again, the committee itself, the applicants, the objectors, and the Senior Planning Officer with a subdued Arnold Landon beside him.

There were two essential differences from the previous meeting, however: a considerably larger number of members of the public had entered the committee room, and Professor John Fisher had clearly made up what differences he might have had with Charles Burke because he was now seated beside the solicitor, Mr Farnum.

'I'm afraid,' the Senior Planning Officer had confided to Arnold, 'you've brought this down upon our heads!'

'You mean that Professor Fisher is going to be advising the Rampton-Burke faction?'

'I mean,' the Senior Planning Officer remarked sententiously, 'that there is truth in the saying that all men have their price. I went over to see Professor Fisher on another matter—the Hexham Church proposal, which, incidentally, you had better deal with immediately this planning matter is completed—and he received me rather coolly. I can't quite make out what it's all about. I imagine you rather . . . ah . . . ruffled Professor Fisher the other evening in that *Northern Lights* programme. I'm not quite sure what you did to his professional ego, but you've done something to him. You are *not* his most popular person.' Nor are you mine, the Senior Planning Officer added wordlessly, with a look.

'But that still doesn't explain why Professor Fisher should actually step over into their camp.'

'*Their* camp?' The Senior Planning Officer admonished Arnold with another withering look. 'That suggests *we* are in the other camp. But we are the professionals—we maintain a dignified impartiality . . . which does not, in my view extend to television appearances.'

Arnold ignored the comment. 'But that's my point,' he urged. 'I thought Professor Fisher would be adopting a similar stance. As an uncommitted academic historian he has a reputation for integrity to uphold. If he is now actually acting as Charles Burke's adviser . . .'

'Quite so.'

'And the last time I saw them,' Arnold added, 'they were near to blows.'

'Hmmm. I heard a whisper about that. But you are clearly not a man of the world, Arnold. The fact is, a . . . *person* . . . such as Mr Burke is fully aware that there are many other ways of skinning a cat than by using a pick-handle.' The Senior Planning Officer smiled to himself: that was rather good. A pick-handle.

'I don't understand,' Arnold said woodenly.

'When I went to see him, Professor Fisher was not inclined to explain his new stance in this matter, but there were a few hints dropped. It seems that Mr Charles Burke . . . ah . . . regretted his physical attack upon

Professor Fisher after the interview. Indeed, he suggested they meet to discuss the matter. The upshot was an amicable agreement.'

'Amicable!'

'As I said, Arnold, you are unworldly. You may have heard that as Professor of Mediæval History the good Professor Fisher has certain responsibilities, not least the furtherance and development of his department and the careers of his colleagues? Falling within that general duty comes the more specific one of trying to obtain for the university collection certain mediæval manuscripts shortly to be sold at Sotheby's. Professor Fisher was hoping, I understand, for certain bequests from the Beddowes estates to fall in. I have a suspicion he is no longer as concerned as he was about the Beddowes money.'

'You mean he's getting funds elsewhere?' Arnold said.

'This is my guess. Why else would he be prepared to speak for a man who very recently almost entered into a bout of fisticuffs with him? And why else would he be prepared to put his . . . ah . . . integrity at risk? Mr Charles Burke has *bought* our friend, Arnold, you mark my words.'

And when Arnold caught Professor John Fisher's defiant glance in the committee room he knew that the Senior Planning Officer was right. He also knew that Fisher was aware of what Arnold Landon thought about it.

Mr Farnum of Todd and Mason was on his feet.

'Mr Chairman, I wish to crave the indulgence of this committee to suggest an unusual step. I think we are all aware of the essential difficulty behind this planning application. The issues are quite clearcut in the main, and can be disposed of, I would imagine, without further discussion or expert opinion. That will be for members of

The Colonel looked to the cherubs but they merely smiled back at him unhelpfully. 'All right, let's get on with it.'

Farnum quickly made the arrangements, a chair being placed to one side so he could face the man to be questioned. 'You will appreciate, Chairman, this will not be an adversarial situation, but inquisitorial. For that reason I shall attempt to act with impartiality, but it will be up to the committee itself to draw the relevant conclusions and make the relevant judgments. And I shall, naturally,' he added with a conspiratorial smile, 'be making no speeches.'

He glanced around, satisfied and then called out, 'Professor John Fisher, if you please?'

Arnold trembled; he had hoped he would have had the chance to answer Fisher's question, and now he was going to get it — but not in the manner he had intended.

He listened in growing panic as Farnum questioned the professor of history. His academic qualifications, his university posts, the books he had written, the papers he had read to distinguished gatherings, the research he had undertaken into mediæval history, and Arnold's heart sank. He knew precisely what Farnum would be doing in a little while, asking Arnold the same questions, with obvious results. The Senior Planning Officer sat stiffly in his seat. Arnold could guess what he'd be thinking. A member of the Planning Department would shortly be exposed as an unqualified fool. That would reflect upon the department itself. Arnold was unhappy, and so, he knew, was the Senior Planning Officer.

'Now then, Professor Fisher,' Mr Farnum was saying, 'on what *evidence* are you basing your assessment of the age of the Old Wheat Barn?'

'On the best available evidence.' Fisher's cool glance flicked towards Arnold as though challenging contradiction. 'On the manorial rolls, the tithe rolls, and the parish records.'

'What does this evidence disclose?'

'That the Old Wheat Barn is a typical example of a sixteenth-century structure. It is first mentioned in the parish records in 1541, as I disclosed in my paper, published five or six years ago.'

'Is there any general comment you would wish to make about the building?'

'Merely that it is a common or standard type as these buildings go. There are quite a number of them scattered through the county. I could name perhaps seven such structures immediately; further research would probably disclose a number of others.'

'And this one possesses no *particularly* interesting facet, historically speaking?'

Fisher pursed his lips. 'None.'

'So, in the interests of assisting the committee in reaching a decision as to whether they should make the Old Wheat Barn a listed property, would you be able to make any comment?'

For the first time, Fisher hesitated. Arnold was staring straight at him, and Fisher avoided his eye. 'I . . . I'm not sure I can.'

Farnum was not to be dissuaded; this was Charles Burke's man. 'Professor Fisher, what I am asking for is a statement that might *assist* the committee. You say there are many such buildings in Northumberland?'

'Several.'

'And this one has no particular significance?'

'None.'

'So what would be your opinion as to the necessity for its protection as a listed building?'

Again Fisher hesitated, and Charles Burke leaned forward. The movement caught Fisher's attention. He lifted one shoulder. 'There is no necessity,' he said.

'So,' Farnum said triumphantly, 'you as an expert, a *qualified* expert, would suggest there is no need to protect this . . . ah . . . unexceptionable building?'

Fisher took a deep breath. 'That,' he announced, 'is correct.'

Farnham bowed slightly to the Professor and allowed him to return to his seat. A swift glance towards the chairman, Colonel Summers, and then he was calling Arnold Landon forward.

Arnold got up numbly. He knew he could not match Professor Fisher but that was not the point. Not any longer. Fisher had as good as said they could demolish the barn, and if they did, the work of John of Wetherby would be lost after six hundred years. Fisher should never have even allowed the chance of that happening. Even if he did not believe Arnold he should never, as a scholar and a historian, have gone so far. If there had been the remotest chance of Arnold being right Fisher should have dug his heels in. And Arnold knew he *was* right.

Then, as he caught Fisher's glance he realized that the Professor was thinking along the same lines. Arnold knew Fisher had sold out to the enemy—and Fisher knew it too.

Farnum leaned over Arnold, confidentially. 'Now, Mr Landon, would you tell the committee what degrees you hold and of which university, please.'

'I hold none.'

'None? Then, your professional qualifications?'

'None.'

'Your experience in the field?'

A cold anger began to stir in Arnold's blood. He stared directly at Farnum. 'It depends what you mean.'

'I mean the field of historical research—papers, books, projects, the study of mediaeval history—'

'None.'

Farnum smiled thinly. 'I see. You have made certain . . . ah . . . claims in this room and also, I believe, in the Press and on television which are the subject of dispute between you and Professor Fisher. Do you consider you are *qualified* to dispute with the Professor?'

The anger stirred again. Arnold looked at Fisher; there was something in the man's eyes he could not read. 'I think I am.'

'Really? Do you not consider your lack of formal or classical education, your lack of research background, places you at a severe disadvantage in the making and presenting of reasoned judgments in matters such as this?'

Arnold took a long, deep breath. 'Mr Farnum, I don't see that it sets me at a disadvantage at all. I am a practical man, like my father before me. I have an enquiring mind. A formal education can assist a man but cannot make him what he is not. I consider an educated hand is far better than a string of degrees.'

Farnum was slightly taken aback. 'You . . . er . . . you heard the Professor testify to the age of this timbered building—'

'Mr Farnum,' Arnold interrupted, 'I attach little credence to that sort of judgment. It is not so very long ago that the academic world ascribed all *timbered* buildings of any antiquity at all to the sixteenth or fifteenth century. I believe carbon dating has changed *that* view.'

Professor Fisher's cheeks were stained pink. Farnum cast a swift glance in his direction and then, in control again, said, 'But no carbon dating has been done on the Old Wheat Barn, and so Professor Fisher has reached a certain conclusion. Based on what he describes as the best available evidence.'

'He is wrong.'

'Why?' Farnum pounced.

'Because the best evidence is the building itself. Most of the people who date buildings work, like Professor Fisher, from *secondary* sources—documents. That's because they don't even have the vocabulary to begin to understand what a building can tell them.'

'But you have,' Farnum asked silkily.

'I think so.'

'Where do you keep this . . . vocabulary . . . this knowledge?'

Arnold hesitated, but he had already gone too far to back down now. 'I keep it in my hands and in my head . . . and in my heart.'

There was a short silence in the room. Farnum stared fixedly at Arnold and let the impact of his words seep through the consciousness of all present. At last, with what sounded like a sigh, he repeated, '*Heart* . . . Interesting. On what evidence do you date the Old Wheat Barn in the fourteenth century, Mr Landon?'

'The discovery of a secret nocked lap joint made by John of Wetherby.'

'How did you find it?'

'I . . . I felt it,' Arnold said.

Once again the silence spread throughout the room. 'You *felt* it . . . in semi-darkness I imagine?'

'Yes.'

'Guided by your head . . . or your heart?'

There was open contempt in Farnum's voice now and it struck a wound deep inside Arnold. He knew what he knew, he felt what he felt as his father had known and felt before him. Snide attitudes from people who believed only what they read were infamous, and the impression Farnum was trying to create in this room denigrated the whole of Arnold's life. It was insupportable.

'Mr Farnum. There is nothing you, or Professor Fisher or any other well-qualified academic can tell me about wood. I've lived it, breathed it, smelled it, tasted it since I was a child. It was the passion of my father's life and it has been mine. You may think it incredible that I walked into the Old Wheat Barn and *felt* something different, but that's the way it was. Maybe people like you have moved too far away from the truth ever to recognize it now, but I haven't, and in that barn, whether you like it or not, something of John of Wetherby spoke to me, and I went up there among the rafters and I found it and there's nothing you or Professor Fisher or Mr Burke can do about that, except destroy it.'

He glared around at the silent committee room. Farnum made a nervous gesture with his hand. 'I think—'

'No, let me finish. Professor Fisher has his documents; that's fine. But to know, to understand a building made of timber you have to be completely familiar with the way those timbers were cut, you must know about tools, the edges they create, the thousands of methods of assembling joints. I know about these things and Professor Fisher does not. And no amount of degrees or academic experience will make up for that knowledge.' Arnold took a deep breath, feeling a prickle behind his eyelids. 'I don't suppose I fit into Professor Fisher's academic world. There are times I don't believe I fit into the modern world at all. I can't live easily with pre-set, machined environments, I can't enjoy a life which is packaged and plastic and predictable. There is no real excitement in the world any more, not the kind of excitement my father instilled in me. There's no real contact with the real world, the reality of streams and stones and trees, with the honest materials, the natural materials. They gave us life and we forget them. They are God-given things and we ignore them. Maybe I'm one of Nature's displaced persons; I was born too late; I'm a man out of my time. But my father gave me a reason to live, a reason for existence, and I won't have that derided or destroyed or taken away from me by academic ignorance. When I went in that barn I buried myself in the past in a way the Professor Fishers of this world will never learn to do; I *felt* John of Wetherby's presence; I discovered his work. And there's nothing anyone can say to take that away from me. That building was erected when I say it was because John of Wetherby worked there. I had the proof under my fingers. All my life led up to that moment and the old barn knew it. And if that isn't *scientific* I don't care. And if it doesn't satisfy academic theory, I don't care. I know what I know, and I've touched hands that have stretched across six hundred years of silence. That's all I have to say.' Arnold hesitated, shaken at the realization of his own vehemence.

Seated beside Colonel Summers, Mrs Oldroyd was quietly crying.

3

The Senior Planning Officer called Arnold into his room the following morning. He made no allusion to Arnold's outburst, though he remarked that the committee had been divided and would not be transmitting a decision on the planning application until the following week. Meanwhile there was the Hexham matter to be dealt with.

Then, as Arnold was leaving the office, the Senior Planning Officer said, 'There is one thing, though. I was over at the university this morning, earlier on. Some discussion going on in the History Department. Looks as though it's doubtful whether Fisher will be getting his money out of Burke after all. There was another row between them, it seems.'

'About what?'

'Not sure, dear boy. Maybe Fisher hadn't gone far enough for Burke — though I don't see he could have gone much further other than to actually suggest blowing the barn up in the interests of historical research. No, I suspect it'll not be Fisher's . . . ah . . . performance there. It might be what he intends to do next.'

'What might that be?'

'Haven't the foggiest. I'm not the man's conscience.'

And Fisher had a conscience. Arnold had seen the reflection of it in the Professor's eyes as he had left the committee room when the hearing was yet again adjourned.

Arnold spent the afternoon at Hexham, eating his lunch down by the river and then dealing with the planning application details relating to the church afterwards. He was unable to complete his work, and a further visit was necessary the following day but Arnold did not object to that: Hexham was a town he loved to visit and the Abbey a structure he never ceased to admire.

Next day he finished his work at the church by eleven-thirty. He had parked in the lower part of the town so he was walking slowly down the main street when someone touched his arm. He turned to see Ben Kelvin.

'Hello, Mr Landon.'

'Mr Kelvin! In for business?'

Ben Kelvin nodded. 'A meeting about some sheep I'm thinking of buying — new stock. Saw you in the street, so I thought I'd have a word with you. I'm sorry I missed you when you called — I was back later than I expected. But Alison looked after you all right?'

'Very well indeed,' Arnold assured him.

'Good.' Ben Kelvin paused, frowning. Arnold seemed to detect a certain strain in the man's features, a puffiness under his eyes that might denote a lack of sleep, a slack weariness about his mouth. Kelvin's glance was still sharp, nevertheless, and now he looked keenly and appraisingly at Arnold. 'I wanted to thank you for what you said at the committee meeting.'

Arnold was vaguely flustered; he was not entirely proud of his outburst — it had been somewhat unprofessional. 'I . . . I was only trying to do what was right. But I got a bit . . . carried away.'

'What you said was right,' Kelvin said grimly. 'It needed saying. I don't want Burke or his kind on my doorstep, and I believe that barn should be preserved. Fred Rampton . . . well, it's rough that he won't make some money out of his farm at last, but I can't help that. I just hope what you found up there in the barn will be enough to turn the tide.'

He hesitated, seemed about to say something more, but then ducked his head and walked away. Arnold watched his stocky figure threading its way through the morning shoppers in the high street. He was slightly puzzled: Ben Kelvin's motives for keeping Charles Burke off Rampton Farm were not as clear as Arnold had thought at first instance. The survey Arnold had undertaken showed quite clearly that interference with Newman Farm would be minimal, and the case Kelvin had put up at the first enquiry had necessarily been one concerned with generalities, relating to the environment and way of life at large, rather than any impact upon Newman Farm itself. Yet Ben Kelvin was not easily cast in the role of conservationist. On the other hand, after the discussion with Alison Kelvin, Arnold might have been persuaded to believe that Kelvin was out to spite Fred Rampton, as another battle in the forty-year war that had been waged between them. But now, this morning, there had been a note of compassion in Kelvin's voice when he mentioned Fred Rampton's hopes.

There was one other possibility, of course, Arnold thought, as he remembered again what Alison Kelvin had told him. For years, Ben Kelvin had stood in the window on occasions looking up to the old barn where he had kept tryst with his youthful sweetheart. A man didn't change, radically; Ben Kelvin had been romantic then, so perhaps there was still a buried streak of that same emotion in him now. His main objection to Brandling Leisure Pursuits could well be that they would be destroying the Old

Wheat Barn, and with it a part of his life that he still dreamed about, almost forty years after it all ended.

In a way, Arnold hoped that was the solution. It appealed to his own innate romanticism—even if he had never known the kind of love that could span decades . . . at least, not love for a woman.

When Ben Kelvin was lost to sight, Arnold made his way back to his parked car and drove back to the office in Morpeth.

There was a note on his desk when he returned. It was a request to phone Professor Fisher at the university. Arnold placed the call reluctantly, for he had no great desire to speak to Fisher. He considered the man had betrayed himself as much as anyone by selling his reputation to Charles Burke, and if the deal was now turning sour on him Arnold was not displeased. He was therefore somewhat relieved when he learned that Professor Fisher was not available, having just left the buildings. Arnold left no message.

The following day he worked again in the office on some files the Senior Planning Officer had left him while he was out attending a conference in Durham, but Arnold found it difficult to concentrate. He felt a sense of impending doom descending upon him and he knew it was something to do with the Old Wheat Barn. The decision of the committee had still not been made; but Arnold was certain that now the Professor had put his weight behind Burke's application, the matter was almost cut and dried. The Fenton faction and the slogan of progress would be enough to overcome Colonel Summers and his small entourage and then it would be all over. The bulldozers would move in and the work of John of Wetherby would be consigned to the dust.

By late afternoon Arnold's sense of nervous anticipation had grown so much that he could not sit still. At five-thirty he left his desk, went down to the car park and headed for home. Yet almost without thinking about it he swung left to take the road past Rothbury and across Coquetdale to the Cumbrian border. He did not know why he was going: perhaps it was merely to reassure himself that the Old Wheat Barn was still there.

It was. It still stood foursquare under the lee of the hill with the black clump of trees behind it and Arnold, a half-mile off in the roadway, stared at it for almost half an hour. He made no attempt to go up to the barn or enter it—he would need Fred Rampton's permission and he was in no state of mind to face that man or his truculent nephew. So he just sat and stared for a while and then, with a sigh, he drove back down the narrow lane.

It was almost seven o'clock and he was suddenly hungry: he had taken only an apple for lunch. He passed a pub called the George and he stopped, reversed down the street and into its car park and then went into the lounge bar where there was a small eating area and ordered a steak.

The waitress who served him was small, pretty, plump and, after she had served him, inclined to stare. Arnold ignored her and ate his steak and chips. He glanced up at one point and saw her looking at him and then saying something to the barman, an elderly, massively-paunched man who stood stolidly wiping a pint glass with a pale blue towel. The barman said something in return to the girl and nodded his head in emphasis. Arnold finished his meal and then decided he would have another drink before he took the drive back home to his cottage.

'Half of lager, please,' he asked when he reached the bar counter.

The barman's eyes were like slits in the heavy flesh of his face. They regarded Arnold with a mild curiosity and when the glass of lager was placed in front of him and

Arnold tendered the money the barman said, 'Shirley reckons you're the feller who was on telly the other night, and caused a bit of a stir.'

'Does she?'

'Was you?'

There was an odd note in the barman's voice; it was not belligerence, and not an avid curiosity—but there was a hint of exasperation in it that surprised Arnold. He nodded. 'If she means *Northern Lights*, I suppose it was me.'

He was about to move back to his seat when the barman said, 'Can't see what all the fuss is about, but you seem to keep the pot boilin' around this way.'

'I do?'

'Well, your name does, anyway. Soon as it was mentioned this afternoon it as good as started a quarrel.'

'Somebody mentioned my name in here this afternoon?' Arnold was taken aback: he had not expected the consequences of fame to attach to him as the result of one television programme.

'That's right. You probably know him. He comes in here regular, like most local farmers. Jimmy Rampton.'

Arnold blinked owlishly. He could not imagine why James Rampton would want to discuss Arnold Landon in a pub, unless—'I suppose it was in connection with this planning application,' he said.

'Dunno,' the barman said indifferently. 'Only came in on the tail of it all, you know. When things started to get violent.'

'Violent?'

'Well, bit out of hand, you know. Not *violent*, exactly.' He gave Arnold a sudden glimpse of blackened teeth. 'Not with me behind the bar, you unnerstand. Used to be a boxer, you know. At the Hoppings over in Newcastle regular each year. All comers. Good days, they was. Now . . .' He shrugged with the resignation of an old man gone to fat.

'Who . . . who was James Rampton having . . . an argument with this afternoon?'

'Aaah, it was all a bit stupid, you know. Beer talking, you know how it is. Been a fair over the hill this morning and they came in for a lunchtime drink, though they wouldn't be in normally, like. So there was a bunch of them, mostly farmers, and they got a bit oiled and they started having a discussion of sorts, and then suddenly things got ugly. That's when I went over to get in between them, you knaa.' He looked down at his massive paunch and grinned.

'Get in between who?'

'Well, Jimmy Rampton . . . silly sod . . . and Jack Sorrell. They was squarin' up, but when I stepped in, it was cooled. Still, there's been an edge between them fellars for years. You'll know about it?'

Arnold hesitated; he was disinclined to gossip. 'Not really,' he said reluctantly.

'Years ago, now,' the barman went on, leaning his fleshy elbows on the bar. 'Jack Sorrell used to have a small piece of land of his own those days. But always disputing with Old Fred Rampton. Something to do with water, one time; fences another. Ended up with Jack Sorrell wavin' a shotgun in Fred's face and the result was old Fred, he got Jack up before the magistrates. And Jack, he always was a bit hasty-tempered, he didn't speak right to the beaks and upshot of it all was that Jack did a month inside. And when he came out, well, his farm went to pieces, and he had to give up the tenancy and went to work for Ben Kelvin over at Newman Farm. Never did forgive old Fred, did Jack Sorrell. Mind you, Fred's an old bastard too. Didn't use to be, mind, I can remember him way back. But it was woman trouble soured him.'

'Molly Stavely?' The name was out before Arnold could prevent himself.

The barman raised his eyebrows. 'Aye, that's right.

You knaa, I'd forgotten the name meself . . . But I remember her well enough. Nice little piece, she were, and no doubt about it. Plump, in the right places if you get my meanin', and lively. Aye, lively, she were. Fred's mother had her workin' at the farm and Fred was taken with her, so, old cow as she was, she ordered Molly off the place. Went overnight she did, and never saw hide nor hair of her after that. Fred, silly bastard, went off lookin' for her and mopin' about the place. Should've married around here, and maybe he'd have turned out different.' He paused, considered the matter thoughtfully, and Arnold had the impression he was perhaps drawing upon his own marital experiences. 'No . . .' the barman reconsidered, 'maybe not . . . maybe not, at that.' He shook his head, and his narrow-slit eyes grew vague, as though he was looking back over the years. 'Molly Stavely aye, plump little piece. But . . . there was something about her the last time she came in here . . . it was two days before she got thrown off and did her flit. Something odd, the way she looked, the way she carried herself, a kind of pride and confidence. Maybe she thought she'd nailed old Fred.' He grunted. 'Or Ben Kelvin. If it was *him* she was wrong, 'cause he was married within weeks. Anyway . . .'

'The argument between James Rampton and Sorrell,' Arnold reminded him.

'Oh, aye, that's right. Oh, I think it blew when Jimmy Rampton started shouting about the old barn up on the hill.'

'What about the old barn?'

'Couldn't make out what they were fussin' about an old barn for. But Jimmy was tanked up and he said it was about time they cut through all the red tape and he was going to go up there and burn the bloody thing down and then all their problems would be solved. And Jack Sorrell shouted that was a typical way for Ramptons to face any problems, ride rough-shod over their neighbours, and

then they got to snarlin' at each other like a couple of
dogs, and when their hackles were really up, well, then I
stepped in. Silly sods . . .'

The barman moved away as one of his regulars in the
public bar called for a beer. Arnold went back to his seat
and sipped his lager. The feeling he had had earlier, the
impending sense of doom, it was back with him more
strongly than ever now. Yet he could hardly believe that
James Rampton would be so foolish or so anarchic as to
destroy the Old Wheat Barn, the only possible barrier
between him and, eventually, a large sum of money.

Arnold finished his drink hastily, went out to his car
and drove up into the hills again to sit, looking down to
the Rampton Farm. There were no lights on; no sign of
movement, and up above, below the clump of trees, the
roof of the Old Wheat Barn caught the last rays of the
setting sun, gleaming pale gold against the darkening sky.

It was foolish; James Rampton would never do such a
thing; it had been beer talking, the bravado induced by
alcohol and company.

Feeling vaguely disturbed, Arnold turned his car and
headed home to the solitude of his cottage.

Arnold had no garage. His cottage was located eight miles
north of Morpeth, at the edge of a small village sheltered
by the first rise of the Cheviots, and he was forced to park
his car under the hedge, open to the night skies. The car
that left Gosforth just at that same time had come out of a
large double garage, attached to a mock-Georgian, four-
bedroomed house, however. The driver was a man envied
by his colleagues for his ability, his success, his fame and
his house, but right now he was not a happy man.

The externals, he considered, were not all. It was
important to him, as it was to many other people, that he
should build about him the trappings of success; it was
important that he should be able to demonstrate regu-

larly his quality of intellect. But it was equally important that, from time to time, when he was faced with a reality that he did not understand, he should not walk away from it. He was not yet certain *why* he felt that way, for there was no certain way of recognizing a reality; like truth, reality could have many faces and some were hidden from one man, not from another. Nevertheless, experience demonstrated that one should accept that nothing was absolute, and least of all intellectual determinants—they could shift, move with the added levels of acceptance, knowledge, feeling, belief.

And this was why he nosed his car out of Gosforth, took the road across town to pick up the A69 and drove past the Wylam of George Stephenson and the Corbridge of the Roman Occupation, into the hinterland beyond Hexham towards Haltwhistle and Greenhead and Gilsland.

Striking north then, into the narrower roads and tracks, his mind was still filled with unanswered questions even though something inside him told him the answers. He had always been a man who had obeyed the dictates of his head: his activities had been deliberate, planned, logical and determinedly pragmatic. But as the hills rose dark ahead of him he knew that he was, for the first time in his life, questioning those values that had determined his course. He had never seen them as shibboleths but the longer he drove in the darkness now, the more convinced he became that perhaps he had been wrong. And it had taken a different kind of man, a person he had regarded as inferior to him in every way, to show him the stark emptiness of his own beliefs. Behind him, gleaming in the mirror, he picked out the headlights of another car, travelling faster than his, perhaps with greater knowledge of the terrain.

The hedges on either side of him gave him only occasional glimpses of the darkened hills, black against the pale night sky, and as the road swung and twisted, so the lights behind him were lost in his mirror for long periods. Then, as the track rose into the hills and his destination, the lights were no longer there and he was alone.

He walked the last hundred yards, across the sloping field, until he stood there facing the ancient structure, looming blackly against the blue-black skyline.

Could you feel history? What *were* the realities? Was it right to support historical research by pandering to modern demands for progress? Did the ghost of conscience have any place in the scramble for funds, when that conscience was alight over such a trivial matter—the look in a man's eyes when he feels himself betrayed by another's denial of standards, the ring of a man's words when he spoke of his own beliefs, but beliefs based on *feeling* and practical experience rather than solidly-based research?

And yet, in a sense, the answers had already been given, thrown in Charles Burke's teeth after the last committee meeting, the refusal to lend further support in the destruction of the barn. It had been a turncoat action, the action of an essentially weak man who had no confidence any longer in his own realities when faced by the rock-like faith of another man in his.

But what *were* those realities? Were they here, under the pale stars, under the ancient darkness of the Old Wheat Barn . . . ?

He stepped forward towards the gaping doors and the blackness seemed to welcome him. He plunged his hand into his pocket as he stumbled, drew forth the pocket torch and flicked it on, just as something in the shadows moved. There was one moment when the beam of the torch picked out a man's face, and then it was lost in blackness and pain, a wet, crushing, throbbing pain.

A pain that quickly faded into a numbness and, finally, into nothing.

CHAPTER 4

1

The Senior Planning Officer listened to Arnold with an expression that lengthened in proportion to his mounting horror. He had wanted an uncluttered enquiry and he had obtained, instead, two meetings where not only had difficult matter been introduced against his will, but a degree of *emotion* had been aroused. And now he was being told that discussions and squabbles were taking place in Northumberland and public houses, with threats of arson actually being made.

'Are you sure of all this, Arnold?'

Arnold nodded unhappily. He had not wanted to destroy the Senior Planning Officer's morning peace of mind, but he himself had spent a sleepless night, tossing and turning at the thought of what might have occurred during the hours of darkness. And when he had arrived at the office it was with the conviction that the Senior Planning Officer would have to be informed or else Arnold himself could be described as in dereliction of duty.

'Arson.' The Senior Planning Officer shook his head. 'This really won't do, Arnold. The matter of the planning application is still *sub judice*. We can't have people taking the law into their own hands, in an attempt to forestall the decision that may, or may not be reached by the Planning Committee.' He reached for the telephone on his desk. 'I shall make contact with Mr Rampton immediately. I shall have to lay the law down to him in no uncertain terms. This simply will *not* do!'

Arnold waited, standing in front of the Senior Planning Officer's desk as he rang Rampton Farm. He could hear, faintly, the brrr-brrr of the phone, and he watched as the Senior Planning Officer's face whitened, and tightened.

'There's no answer. You say you went out there last night?'

'Yes, sir.'

'And the barn was intact then?'

'Yes, sir.'

'You should have stayed,' the Senior Planning Officer muttered, almost to himself. 'You really should have stayed or gone down to the farm to warn them, or something.'

'The farm seemed to be deserted, sir. No lights.'

The Senior Planning Officer replaced the telephone and began to chew at his nails nervously. He was proud of his nails; his action now demonstrated to Arnold that crisis was near. Then the Senior Planning Officer calmed, looked at his damaged nails and decided he could not be spared from the office.

'*You'll* have to go out there, Arnold,' he said. 'You'll have to go and take them to task. Lay the law down to them. Explain what might be the penalties for arson.' He looked blank for a moment. 'What *are* the penalties for arson, Arnold—if it's your own property?'

Normally a cautious, rather slow driver, Arnold now forsook old habits and drove quickly out of Morpeth, across country to pick up the military road past Choller-ford and over the straight, uncompromising run to Greenhead. He gave no thought to the Senior Planning Officer's last question: rather, he felt the dread of topping a rise and seeing a stark-ribbed, smoking ruin where the Old Wheat Barn had been. He thought of how last evening the dying rays of the sun had gilded that ancient roof and he pushed his foot down, thrusting the car along the lonely road until he dipped into Greenhead, swung along towards Gilsland and finally headed north on the narrow road leading to Rampton Farm.

There was no smudge of smoke on the mid-morning sky, and when he finally breasted the slope that overlooked Rampton Farm itself and gave him a view of the hill where the Old Wheat Barn stood, he gave out a vast sigh of relief. The Old Wheat Barn still stood.

Arnold realized suddenly that his hands were shaking, the result of a release from the tension that had been building up inside him ever since he had risen from his bed that morning. He slowed now, stopped, and sat there for a while looking across to the barn where it stood in the hazy sunshine. Then, recalling the words of the Senior Planning Officer, he started the car again, to drive down to Rampton Farm.

It had to be made quite clear to the Ramptons that they should not take the law into their own hands.

The yard was deserted and, if anything, more dilapidated in general appearance than Arnold remembered. He got out of the car and one of the two dogs he had seen previously came slinking around the corner, eyeing him nervously and snarling with a distinct lack of confidence, ready to turn tail and run if he as much as lifted a boot. Arnold walked across to the door and hammered at the knocker. The sound reverberated inside, just as though the whole house was empty.

Arnold waited, then knocked again. And again.

At last, from deep within the farmhouse he heard someone shouting indistinctly. Arnold waited. After several minutes there was the sound of someone walking along the flagged corridor; there was the rattling of a bolt and the door opened.

James Rampton stood in the open doorway in a stained, open-necked shirt and baggy slacks. He was unshaven and his eyes were red-rimmed as though he had slept badly. He stared at Arnold with a massive lack of comprehension, and it took several seconds for Arnold's identity to register with him. 'Whaddyou want?' he finally managed to say, thick-tongued and bad-tempered.

Stiffly Arnold replied, 'I'd like to have a few words with you . . . and with your uncle.'

'Fred's not here.'

'Where is he?'

'Haven't the faintest.'

Arnold hesitated. 'The Senior Planning Officer rang the farm from the office this morning. There was no answer.' When James Rampton made no reply, Arnold asked angrily, 'Why didn't you answer it?'

'Because I was flat out,' Rampton replied.

'You could have saved me a journey.'

'Big deal. I didn't ask you to come out here.' James Rampton paused then, as though searching his mind for something, turning out drawers of his memory, peering into dark, unpleasant corners. 'Wass this about, anyway?'

'I came out to see if the barn was all right.'

'The barn?' Rampton's puzzlement seemed genuine, and then something else crawled into his eyes, a doubt, an uncertainty that bothered him. 'Whaddyou mean, see if it's all right?'

Arnold took a deep breath. 'I understand there was something of an altercation at the George, yesterday lunchtime. You were heard to make certain remarks, utter threats about burning down the Old Wheat Barn.'

James Rampton scowled. 'You get around, Mr Landon—or is it just that news travels fast? All right, so there was some shouting went on at the George. What if . . .' His voice died away and he flicked a look past Arnold to the hill above the farm. 'You came out to make sure that I hadn't *fired* the damn thing!'

'Something like that,' Arnold said sternly.

Rampton took a deep breath and fingered the stubble on his chin. 'Don't remember too much about it. It would've been whisky talk, thass all. Don't remember much at all about yesterday, as a matter of fact. Left the George and had a meal and then I was back at the Running Mare by six. Took on a skinful there, I can tell you! How the hell I made it back to the farm beats me. 'Cept I seem to remember it wasn't too late. Eleven, maybe. Anyway . . .'

'I think I'd better make it clear,' Arnold interrupted. 'The application still lies before the committee and it would not be taken kindly if there was anything done which . . . interfered with the *status quo*. You made certain remarks in the pub yesterday; I would advise that you take no such action as you threatened there. Arson is a serious offence and there would be a prosecution, take my word for it. So if you or your uncle—'

'The hell with you, you pompous prig!' James Rampton hawked and spat venomously. 'I told you, that was whisky talking down at the George. And Fred and me, we got no plans to fire any bloody old barn. But that don't mean we're not sick about the whole thing, about you and your stupid blasted snooping for joints, for God's sake. Aye, and about that snivelling professor too.'

'What about Professor Fisher?' Arnold asked in surprise. 'I thought—'

'To hell with what you thought! Mr Burke has told us—we can't rely on the little bastard. If I could get my hands on him . . .' Rampton peered at Arnold hazily, perhaps thinking back to his threats of the previous afternoon and now considering it better if he held his tongue. 'Why don't you shove off back to your bloody office now, hey? Your precious barn is safe; nobody's laid a finger on it.'

'I'd like to be sure of that.'

'Go to hell!'

'You'll pass my message to your uncle when he gets back?'

James Rampton uttered an expletive.

'And I'd like to go up and inspect the barn,' Arnold said firmly.

'Whaffor?'

'To be certain nothing's been done to it.'

The uncertainty was back in James Rampton's face, creeping like a wavering shadow across his eyes, touching his mouth; he hesitated for a long moment, and glanced involuntarily up at the hill. 'I don't see why—'

'Just to be sure.'

' 'Strespass,' Rampton affirmed weakly.

'That's why I'm asking formal permission.'

'Fred'll . . .' James Rampton still hesitated, scraping his hand against his chin nervously. 'I don't know . . .'

Arnold waited, and the tension grew between him and Fred Rampton's nephew. At last, with a snarling cough James Rampton turned away, back into the house. 'Aaah, do what the hell you like!'

The door to the farmhouse slammed behind him.

Arnold was not certain he'd handled the matter in the way the Senior Planning Officer would have wished but there was nothing more he could do about that. It was clear that any further attempt to rouse James Rampton would be met with failure, and if Fred Rampton was not available, the only thing left to do was to undertake a reconaissance of the Old Wheat Barn to make sure that, in spite of his denials, James or his uncle had not made an attempt to remove from their path the one thing that might yet prevent approval of the planning application. As he walked from the yard Arnold wondered vaguely where Fred Rampton had gone.

There was no point in taking the car and driving back down the track, into the lane and then swinging around to breast the hill. It was simpler to leave his own car here and walk out of the hollow, cut across the field and take the long, rising walk up towards the trees and the barn. A quick look around and then he could collect the car, make his way back to Morpeth in an easier frame of mind. And the Senior Planning Officer would be pleased that nothing serious had in fact occurred.

Arnold walked over the tussocky grass and began the climb. It had rained at some time during the night, and the grass had retained the moisture so his shoes were wet and dark-stained within minutes. They were town shoes, not suited to walking, but then, Arnold hadn't expected to be crossing fields this morning.

As he climbed the hill he caught a glint from the track running parallel to his walk, in the roadway up which he would otherwise have driven his car. Twenty yards on he could see that someone had parked a car there, against the hedge. He wondered whether it might be Fred Rampton and almost involuntarily he quickened his pace, heading rapidly for the Old Wheat Barn.

At the top of the hill he looked back and doubted whether the car truly belonged to Fred Rampton. If the state of Rampton Farm was anything to go by it was highly unlikely the car would be Rampton's: it was too big, too expensive, and too clean.

Puzzled, Arnold looked across to the Old Wheat Barn. He could make out no sign of life. Slowly he walked forward, his eyes searching the structure of the barn, the roof, the walls for any sign of damage, any hint that James or his uncle might have been up to any sabotage there. He could see no sign of disturbance of any kind — but in looking upwards he was almost upon the untidy bundle that lay beside the doors of the barn before he saw it.

Arnold stopped. He stared and something moved in his stomach, the first churning of presentiment, the first stir of fear. Slowly he walked forward until he was only feet from the bundle.

It was the body of a man.

He was lying on his side, his arms half covering his face, his legs spread at awkward angles. He was not dressed as formally as the occasions when Arnold had seen him before: dark trousers, a roll-neck sweater and a casual jacket. His eyes were open but sightless, and underneath his head there was a dark stain that had started to spread, but had stopped, soaking into the earth some time during the night.

Arnold considered he should perhaps have gone forward, sought a pulse, but he did not. He knew Professor John Fisher was dead.

He turned almost mechanically. The knot of fear had hardened in his stomach now: he felt the hilltop was alive with something menacing; he felt someone was up there among the trees, watching him. The fear was translated into a panic that rose to his brain, threatening to engulf reason. He began to walk away. But not back to Rampton Farm. Instead, he headed away from it, towards the hedge and the road and he broke into a run.

A few minutes later he was hammering on the door of Newman Farm, the breath whistling in his chest, his mouth loose and jerking.

The door opened and there stood Alison Kelvin. Her eyes widened with shock as she saw the state Arnold was in but she did not begin to shake until she heard his words.

'I must use your phone . . . I must call the police. The Professor . . . someone's murdered Professor Fisher at the Old Wheat Barn!'

2

The next few days were agonizing in their uncertainty. Arnold went to the office as usual and after the first, almost violent waves of curiosity when all the secretaries in the building seemed to want to get a look at him, there was an inevitable reaction when everyone seemed to want *not* to see him, or be seen talking to him, and he began to realize what it was like to be a pariah.

Even the Senior Planning Officer, the rock against whom so many waves broke, was affected by the situation. On the first morning he drew Arnold into his office, gave him a sympathetic cup of coffee and requested that Arnold give him a verbal report. The story of the visit to Rampton Farm was easily told; the relating of the discovery of Professor Fisher's body was less easy because the prickling feeling, the feeling that he had been watched from the trees, returned to Arnold as he spoke, but could be discussed coherently enough. It was the rest of the report that proved the most difficult.

It might have been due to the fact that Arnold had been in a state of shock. Nevertheless, his memory of the hours after the discovery were vague in the extreme. could clearly recall the shock on Alison Kelvin's face when he had blurted out the news to her on the doorstep; he was able to admire still the control she had shown thereafter in making him a cup of strong tea while he had called the police. But their conversation thereafter, during the hour while they waited for the police to arrive, was lost to him. He had sat there, numbly, unbelieving, and hardly aware of his surroundings, unable to excise from his mind the image of the body of Professor Fisher lying outside the Old Wheat Barn.

Some ten minutes before the arrival of the police there was the sound of a Land-Rover driving into the yard. Alison had made her way out to meet it, trembling and on the verge of tears. A few minutes later Ben Kelvin had come in, his mouth sagging, his eyes alarmed.

'What the hell happened?'

He had stood staring out of the window, up towards the Old Wheat Barn in the way he must have done over the years, watched covertly by his wife, and Arnold had told him as much as he knew.

'But what was he *doing* up there?' Kelvin had asked with a surprising fierceness, as though he resented the Professor having come anywhere near the barn. Perhaps it was because he had seen him as an enemy over the planning application, but the almost desperate vehemence of his remark had surprised Arnold. There was no adequate answer Arnold could give. Ben Kelvin turned to his wife and put one arm around her shoulders solicitously. 'I'm sorry I wasn't here when Mr Landon came with the news.'

She nodded, pathetically grateful for the sign of affection, and Arnold wondered briefly from her reaction whether her married life had seen many such examples of overt regard. Ben Kelvin did not seem to be a demonstrative man; indeed, there was something of the tightly coiled spring about him, a reluctance ever to be free in personal terms, and the news that Landon brought had certainly done nothing to release his inner tensions on this occasion.

'I had to go over to Carlisle yesterday,' he explained to Arnold, 'so I wasn't home last night. The meeting was an evening farmers' meeting, so I stayed at an hotel — got bored this morning so didn't wait for all the business to be finished. Some of these Cumbrian farmers, they talk and talk . . . Anyway, I'm glad I came back early now.' He glanced at his wife, and then looked back out of the window again, thinking, perhaps, that while his wife had been alone in the farmhouse, a murderer had been standing up there in the darkness, overlooking Newman Farm.

'Did you see Fred Rampton this morning?' Ben Kelvin had asked abruptly.

'No. Just James . . . he said his uncle was away.'

'I half expected to see him at Carlisle,' Kelvin said thoughtfully, drawing his brows together in a frown, 'but he didn't turn up . . .'

Any further conversation was then brought to an end

by the arrival of the police.

They had sent one car up the lane to take a look at the body; Arnold had been questioned briefly, statements had been taken from Alison and Ben Kelvin, and then what seemed like a fleet of cars had been parked in the lane and forensic experts were swarming with police officers over Fisher's car, the lane, the field and the barn itself, while a small screening tent was erected about the body of the dead professor.

And when Arnold was finally allowed to leave and walk back down to collect his car from Rampton Farm the police were down there too, and James Rampton was in the yard, white-faced, talking to them.

Three days slipped past and the only information Arnold obtained about the death of Professor Fisher was gleaned from newspaper reports. No attempt was made to contact him and he had no communication with the Kelvins or the Ramptons. The atmosphere in the office was still edgy, occasional groups of conversationalists falling silent when he walked past, but eventually he began to ignore their reactions, and the pattern of work began to fall into its usual, natural situation.

Until the phone rang on his desk and a pleasant voice, having identified itself as belonging to Chief Inspector Tudor, asked if he would mind walking along to Morpeth Headquarters for a chat about the death of Professor Fisher. Arnold did mind; the prospect appalled and frightened him; he said he didn't mind, and would come immediately.

'Not necessary, boy, not immediate. This afternoon, say, about two o'clock, is it?'

Arnold promised to be there.

He turned up early, and it was a mistake. It was some ten minutes before he was due and he was shown into a small waiting-room on the first floor. The room was already occupied and the other occupant was not pleased to see him. It was Fred Rampton.

He was sitting in the corner of the room, bolt upright, his craggy features more dissatisfied than ever. It was obvious that he too had been called in to help the police with their enquiries, and it seemed as though Chief Inspector Tudor was running a little late with his appointments. But Rampton's disillusioned old eyes sparkled when they saw Arnold; the sparkle contained nothing that was welcoming in it, however—the eyes betrayed an animosity, as though Fred Rampton considered it was all Arnold's fault that he found himself here at Morpeth Headquarters.

Which in one sense, Arnold considered, was probably true. If Arnold had not discovered the secret nocked lap joint of John of Wetherby in the Old Wheat Barn, Professor Fisher would almost certainly never have come near the barn. And died under its walls . . . but did his death have anything to do with Arnold's discovery?

Arnold shook himself mentally—he had not till now even tried to associate the two. Indeed, he had not even enquired within himself into the reason for Fisher's death. It had seemed such an enormity in itself, such an unpredictable, inexplicable, horrific situation that the basic realities behind it, the fact that someone had killed Fisher for a particular reason, these were matters Arnold had not addressed his mind to—and he did not want to start now.

'Hello, Mr Rampton,' he said nervously and sat down. Fred Rampton grunted an unintelligible reply, and looked away. He was nursing his right hand; Arnold could see that the old man had his knuckles swathed in a dirty-looking bandage, and he wondered vaguely what accident had caused the injury on the farm.

They sat there for perhaps ten minutes, without speaking, until finally the door of the waiting-room

opened and a tall, portly man in a worn grey suit stood
there smiling at them. He had a friendly, chubby face,
red-cheeked, with tiny blue eyes and his hands were large,
inclined to wave in emphasis to his words.

'Ah, I'm sorry to have kept you waiting, gentlemen.
Running a bit behind, we are, but you know each other
anyway, don't you, so I don't suppose you minded
waiting? Could always have a chat, like, isn't it?' He
smiled benignly, and Arnold had a vague suspicion,
probably an unjust one, about the Welsh accent that so
clearly came across to them. 'Still, if you wouldn't mind
coming along to my office, Mr Rampton? I'll see you soon
as I can, Mr Landon.'

He walked away into the corridor as Fred Rampton
rose, bad-temperedly, to follow him. Rampton made no
attempt to close the door behind him so Arnold walked
across after him. In the corridor, waiting for the lift
because of his wife's condition, was Ben Kelvin, with
Alison standing beside him. They were both staring at
Chief Inspector Tudor and the angry figure of Fred
Rampton walking past them.

Alison seemed vaguely alarmed, a shadow of anxiety
flickering in her eyes as though she expected some scene
between the two neighbouring farmers who had been so
out of sorts with each other for almost forty years. Arnold
could not see Fred Rampton's features, but the set of his
shoulders and the belligerence of his walk told their own
tale.

As for Ben Kelvin, his face was stiff, his features
inscrutable. He was staring fixedly at Fred Rampton as
though weighing something up in his mind, but otherwise
his face was a blank, completely without expression, his
eyes almost vacant in their stare. The hostility over the
years, Arnold knew, had come from the dissatisfied Fred
Rampton: Arnold guessed that Ben Kelvin had come to
terms with the relationship many years ago and was now

unaffected by it, and yet he was not prepared to ignore Fred Rampton. Even now, if Fred Rampton had spoken, something might have softened in Ben Kelvin's face.

Fred Rampton did not speak.

Arnold closed the door and went back to his seat. It was almost twenty minutes before Chief Inspector Tudor came back to the waiting-room. Fred Rampton had already gone. In his office, Chief Inspector Tudor waved Arnold to the chair that was placed to face squarely the desk behind which Tudor settled his portly bulk. Tudor offered Arnold a cigarette but when he refused, did not take one himself; instead, he picked up a pencil and began to nibble the end of it thoughtfully.

'You a local man, Mr Landon? No? Yorkshire, hey? Ah well, not a bad place to be though, is it? From Wales myself — as you'll have noticed. Always notice, they do. Once asked, I did, is it the way I talk? No, this bloke said, it's the way you *walk*.' Tudor grinned, eyeing Arnold, who managed only a sickly smile.

'Don't worry,' Tudor soothed, 'I just want to ask a few questions to underline things you said in your statement, the day you found the body.' The Welsh accent was less pronounced now, and Arnold's earlier guess had been right: Tudor was inclined to emphasize it occasionally, to lull the hearer. A man with a heavy accent was rarely regarded as sharp, or intelligent.

'I . . . I think I said everything I knew in the statement,' Arnold said.

'Maybe, maybe . . . but second thoughts sometimes help, don't they? Anyway, let's go over it again, shall we?'

They went carefully over Arnold's statement, but Arnold was unable to add anything new to what he had already told the police. Nodding, Tudor leaned back in his chair, puffed out his red cheeks and inspected the end of his chewed pencil. 'Fair enough. Stands up all right. Let me ask you something else now, all right?' The little eyes suddenly snapped up to Arnold. 'What do you reckon the Professor was *doing* up there at the barn that night, Mr Landon?'

Arnold's mouth was dry. He shook his head. 'I . . . I've no idea.'

'I just wondered whether he'd gone up there to meet someone. You, for instance.'

'Me? Why should he expect to see me there?'

'Well, now . . .' Chief Inspector Tudor drew forward the file in front of him and flicked it open. 'You . . . you and this university professor, you been having a bit of a tussle, like, haven't you?'

'I wouldn't have put it quite like that,' Arnold demurred.

'No, *I* put it like that,' Tudor said but did not smile. 'I understand you didn't see eye to eye about something, that this was public knowledge from a planning committee meeting and also a television broadcast. Right?'

'Yes, but—'

'So, maybe he thought you might be up there at the barn that night?'

'He would have no reason to think so. And that time of night—'

'But you'd been up there earlier, anyway, hadn't you?' Tudor demanded.

Arnold hesitated. As Tudor waited, Arnold's mind spun back to that day in the office: he had been disturbed, upset by some sixth sense that warned him of impending doom. He struggled to get the words out. 'Well, yes, I had but it . . . it was just a casual visit.'

'Casual?' Chief Inspector Tudor raised sarcastic eyebrows and a slight edge crept into his tone. 'You're suggesting to me that at the end of a day's work in the office, before you go home for a meal, you're inclined to take a *casual* drive of . . . what . . . thirty miles there, and back? Try again, Mr Landon.'

'It's difficult to explain.'

'Try hard,' Tudor said soothingly, as though he spoke to a recalcitrant child.

'I . . . I just felt . . . *odd*.' Arnold saw the detective's frown begin and he went on desperately, 'I couldn't concentrate all afternoon. I had a sort of feeling that something might happen to the barn . . . *have* happened to it. It was almost automatic to drive out there to . . . to . . .'

'To see if the barn was still intact.' Tudor regarded him gravely. 'The barn is important to you?'

The answer was obvious. 'The barn . . . what it contains . . . yes.'

Tudor nodded slowly, looking again at the file. 'How important?' There was a short silence; as it lengthened, Arnold felt his collar grow damp. 'Important enough to turn to violence to protect it?'

Arnold could not bring himself to essay a reply.

'Where do you live, Mr Landon?'

'Outside Morpeth.'

'House?'

'Cottage.'

'Alone?'

'Yes.'

'So we have only your word for it that you returned home to your cottage after your *brief* visit to the barn; only your word for it that you didn't stay there, or had an assignation with Fisher; or met him there by surprise and had an argument—'

'This talk is foolish!'

Tudor regarded him owlishly. 'Maybe. But it *is* only your word.'

'Yes . . . but I stopped at the George for a meal before driving home—'

'*If* you drove home . . .' Tudor consulted the file again. 'You were certainly out there again in the morning.'

'On the instructions of my superior.'

'He told you to go to the farm . . . Rampton Farm.'

'Yes, but—'

'But you had a *feeling* again, about the barn,' Tudor interrupted scathingly.

'You're twisting everything!'

Chief Inspector Tudor sighed. 'Aye, maybe, maybe. Occupational hazard. Cup of coffee?'

Weakly, Arnold assented. He felt a little light-headed: it seemed that Tudor actually considered he might be in some way responsible for Fisher's death! He was alone in the room and his hands were shaking slightly, his head filled with spinning, confused thoughts. He heard Tudor saying something in the corridor outside and then the big policeman had returned, and was easing his bulk into the chair behind the desk once again. 'Ahhh, right, the coffee will be here in a moment. So you . . . er . . . you haven't any idea what our deceased friend might have been doing up there that night, then?'

Arnold wasn't sure: something danced in his mind, a possible reason for Fisher's presence, but it depended upon the kind of feeling that Tudor had already sneered at, the expression in a man's eyes across a crowded committee room. Arnold shook his head dumbly.

'Pity. Never mind, is it? Let's get on.' Tudor leaned back in his seat again, relaxing, teasing once more at the end of the pencil with his teeth. 'You went up at the direction of your Senior Planning Officer to see the Ramptons that morning. What was that about?'

'It was merely to warn them that since the matter of the barn was *sub judice* in the planning application they would be ill-advised to do anything . . . precipitate.'

Tudor chuckled. 'Aye, I know what you mean. I remember a builder on the Gower coast; knocked down a stately home to build a caravan site. Hell to pay there was . . . but he got away with it. Fred Rampton wasn't in when you called.' It was a statement, not a question, but Tudor watched him keenly as he awaited the answer. Arnold shook his head. 'No, I saw James but he told me his uncle was away.'

'Know where?'

'No.'

'Hmmm.' Almost dreamily, Tudor said as though to himself, 'Across at Newcastle, he claimed. Auction sale . . . but didn't buy anything. And no one there he knew. Booked in at the Turk's Head. Keep their doors open all night, they do . . .' There was a short silence, and then Tudor asked, 'And James Rampton, did he tell you what time he got back to Rampton Farm?'

'I think he said about eleven. He'd been drinking.'

'Forensic say Fisher died around about that time. You . . . er . . . you say the Ramptons had no cause to love Fisher? I mean, you think they disliked him enough to—'

'I can't draw any such conclusions,' Arnold said desperately, 'because I haven't the faintest idea how they regarded him. In fact, he was supportive of their planning application and I would have thought—'

'Ah yes, but I heard a rumour,' Tudor intervened, 'that maybe he'd changed his mind.'

Arnold considered the matter. Reluctantly he said, 'I had heard something of the sort, but nothing formal—'

'It would have been enough to get James Rampton real mad at Fisher, wouldn't it? Or his uncle too, for that matter.'

Tudor stared at Arnold but when he would not be drawn Tudor smiled and threw down his pencil. 'Aye, well, not a very productive line of thinking, is it . . . ? Ah, the coffee.'

The trim policewoman brought in two mugs of coffee; it was strong and unsugared. Tudor caught his glance and patted his stomach. 'Got to watch my figure, see. Now then, where were we?'

'I'm not sure where we are, Chief Inspector,' Arnold
was bold enough to reply. 'It seems to me you're thinking
aloud and asking me questions I could not possibly
answer.' He sipped his coffee. 'I don't see in what way I
can possibly help you, beyond my original statement.'

'First at the scene of the crime, though, boy, weren't
you? That means a *degree* of involvement; the kind of
involvement that might have placed you in possession of
facts which you haven't recognized yet as important and
maybe never will, until some casual question from some
clodhopping copper like me draws them out.'

Duly admonished, Arnold sipped his coffee again.
Tudor watched him for a moment. 'You're different from
these others, aren't you, Mr Landon?'

Warily, Arnold asked, 'Different? In what way?'

'I don't know. I'm not a perceptive man, but I get the
idea you don't *fit* too well. I'm not sure where . . . but
somewhere, you don't fit. This passion of yours, is that it?
Old joints and all that?'

Arnold's tone was stiff. 'I have an interest in such
things. I don't know why it makes me different.'

And yet he felt different; he had said as much in the
committee hearing. Tudor would have received a report
on that hearing. A slow stain of colour marked Arnold's
cheeks, embarrassment in being caught out in a half-lie.
Tudor grimaced. 'Don't get me wrong, Mr Landon. I'm
not criticizing, or complaining. But a man who has an
obsession, he gets to develop different senses, sees people
in a different light very often. I just wonder about you.
Take the Kelvins, now: what d'you think about them?'

'They are very pleasant people.'

'You know he married her for her money, don't you?'

The brutal comment startled Arnold; it also annoyed
him. He raised his head, stared fixedly at Tudor. '*I* know
it; so does she.'

Tudor's eyes dilated slightly, then he nodded reflectively. 'Aye . . . I wondered about that. And I believe it. She's a woman of character and tenacity, seems to me.'

'They've had a happy marriage.'

'Why not?' Tudor challenged. 'She's got what she wanted—and so did he. But you're defensive about them.'

'I like them.'

'The Ramptons don't.'

Arnold almost replied with the uncharitable thought that the Ramptons seemed to like few people and were disliked in their turn.

'Mrs Kelvin was alone when you ran there in the morning,' Tudor said. 'And had been alone the previous night.'

'I understand Mr Kelvin went to Carlisle.'

'And stayed the night.' Chief Inspector Tudor smiled and shook his head. 'Odd, isn't it? A bloke who shouldn't have been there gets killed. Two blokes whom one would have *expected* to be there weren't—and the third was dead drunk at the time. Or so he claims. And somebody else who *might* have been there, and *was* earlier, claims he'd gone home. To his lonely bed.'

'Chief Inspector—'

'No, never mind, I was just thinking out loud, and generally bewailing my lot. Finish your coffee, Mr Landon, and then you'll be free to leave.' He stared moodily at his own cup for a little while. Then he added, 'Even so, it would help if you *could* find some confirmation for your whereabouts after, say, nine-thirty that night. I feel uneasy at the thought of having four characters, with a reason to be in the vicinity, without alibis for the time in question.' He hesitated, then looked up at Arnold. 'There's one thing though—you haven't asked me the question the others did. Each of them, like clockwork.'

'I don't understand.'

'They each of them asked me how Fisher was killed.'
Tudor said slowly.

'I . . .' Arnold hesitated. To raise the question had never
occurred to him. It was enough to know appallingly, that
Professor John Fisher was dead. Murdered. The method
used was an obscene irrelevance as far as Arnold was
concerned; he had known Fisher briefly, and he had seen
the man's eyes in that committee hearing. He wanted no
details of his death: finding the body had been more than
enough.

'Not curious?' Tudor asked.

'No.'

'I'll tell you, anyway. It's odd, you see. I'm not sure the
murderer intended to kill him. Or at least, kill him that
way. The way it looks, Fisher was approaching the barn,
using a flashlight. He must have seen his killer: maybe
they'd arranged to meet, maybe not; maybe they talked,
maybe not. But at some point of time the killer grabbed
Fisher by the wrist and elbow, and dragged him forward.
Fisher wasn't a big man. Off balance, he came hurtling
forward, and crashed into the wall of the barn, the
timber of the doorway support.'

Ancient timber, almost petrified after centuries; hard
as iron. Arnold blinked.

'A normal man,' Tudor continued, 'it would have laid
him out, certainly; possibly a fracture. But Fisher . . . egg-
shell skull, it seems. Bad fracture; splinters of bone . . . But
there you are. Act of violence. Death. Murder.'

Arnold finished his coffee in a gulp and rose to go.
Tudor remained seated behind his desk, watching him
appraisingly. 'Aye, the others asked. You never did.' He
smiled thinly, but without humour. 'Question is, what am
I to make of your lack of curiosity, Mr Landon?'

The menace and the accusation in the question seemed
to cling to Arnold's clothes for the rest of the day: an
odour of suspicion.

3

Arnold remained disturbed by his visit to the police headquarters during the whole of the next two days and his work began to suffer. The Senior Planning Officer regarded him with a cautious eye but kept his distance, and although he was clearly aware of Arnold's lack of concentration, he made no comment about it.

Arnold was not certain whether he felt grateful for the way the Senior Planning Officer kept his distance or not: the fact was, his own mind was so confused that he was not able to decide whether he wanted a confidant or a father confessor. Chief Inspector Tudor had, in some odd way, half-convinced Arnold that he had played a major part in the killing of Professor Fisher: Arnold felt guilty, but did not know what he felt guilty about.

There was one other thing that bothered him in relation to his interview with Tudor. Arnold had a vague feeling that he had not done himself justice. The way the questions had been thrown at him, he had been unable to explain himself properly—it was as though he was being deliberately tested, and pushed along preconceived paths. He felt he had left certain suspicions in Tudor's mind which could have been cleared up without too much trouble. Additionally, there was something else niggling at him, as far as the information he had given Tudor was concerned.

There was something he had omitted to tell Tudor, but there was no way he could tell whether it was important or not. There *had* been an omission, but he could not think what it might have been. It was only when the Senior Planning Officer came in to complain to him that he remembered.

The Senior Planning Officer was upset.

'All I wanted was a clear, uncluttered decision-making session,' he complained. 'Instead, what do we get? First, some fairly weak objections from local farmers like Mr Kelvin—weak, but emotional. Then you come up, Arnold, with this story about this . . . joint of historical interest. I agree it's important, but it does cause us problems. I would have preferred, of course, if you hadn't pressed the matter once Professor Fisher pronounced, but you did, so . . . And then there's the matter of Professor Fisher's death.'

The Senior Planning Officer made it sound as though the murder was a deliberately conceived inconvenience to the Planning Department rather than a tragic occurrence with horrific overtones. He sighed, as Arnold waited in trepidation, guessing there was more. 'And now, the final straw,' the Senior Planning Officer announced.

'What's happened, sir?' Arnold asked.

'The next planning committee meeting, adjourned to consider further the Rampton planning application and your own submission regarding the barn,' the Senior Planning Officer intoned lugubriously, 'is not to be held at the committee room allocated. They will meet there, but then the chairman wants the meeting to convene at the Old Wheat Barn!'

Arnold gaped. 'But what's the point—'

'The *point* of it,' the Senior Planning Officer said with a hint of malice, 'is that you've got some of them so worked up about the possibility of this ancient joint of yours that they want to go view it and the barn *in situ*, so to speak. At least, that's what Colonel Summers told me—it's necessary to view the whole situation, he said. Get the complete picture before we commit ourselves.' The Senior Planning Officer looked distastefully at his cuffs, as though seeking for errant smuts. 'I fear the objective is much more reprehensible.'

'I don't understand, sir.'

'It's not that they want to view the site of the secret nocked lap joint in my opinion,' the Senior Planning

Officer intoned. 'They want to view the site of the murder of Professor Fisher! Quite reprehensible. Pandering to basic and vulgar curiosity. However . . . I am instructed by the chairman of the committee to make the necessary application to the police—and I think they'll be *quite* wrong if they accede to the request, incidentally—and, since I am merely an officer and not a member, I must follow my instructions. So, Arnold, I shall be out of the office for the next hour or so, and you know where I shall be. Morpeth Police Headquarters.'

He swept out before Arnold could say another word. And after he had gone Arnold realized he could have taken a message to Chief Inspector Tudor, to explain something Arnold had not managed to get across during his interview.

For Arnold now recalled that while Chief Inspector Tudor had asked him about his going to Rampton Farm that morning, he had not been able to explain to Tudor *precisely* why he had done so. He had not managed to tell him that the warning he was delivering to James Rampton had become necessary because of what Arnold had heard in the George Hotel—the fact that James Rampton had been talking about setting fire to the Old Wheat Barn.

But then, Arnold considered after a while, it probably wasn't very important anyway—no more important than the fact that Jack Sorrell had a grudge against the Ramptons. If one questioned deeply enough, one would receive a whole mass of irrelevant information, such as those two facts. The Chief Inspector was a professional; he knew what he was doing; his questions were professionally designed to elicit only that information that was essential to the solving of the case before himn. Chief Inspector Tudor would probably not welcome Arnold sending such messages down to him through third parties, or at all. On reflection, Arnold considered, it was as well the Senior

Planning Officer had gone from the office before Arnold recalled what he had not told Tudor.

It probably wouldn't have helped in any case.

Ten minutes later, one of the clerks from the office below rang upstairs to Arnold's office. 'There's a gentleman here wanting to see someone in the Planning Department. I rang the Senior Planning Officer's number but there's no answer.'

'He'll be away from the office for an hour or so,' Arnold advised. 'Did the gentleman have an appointment?'

There was a muffled, garbled sound, then the girl came back on. 'No, no appointment, but it's to do with the Rampton planning application. Shall I send him up?'

Arnold hesitated. 'Well, I suppose so. Direct him to my office, then, will you, please?'

A few minutes later he regretted the invitation, when the door opened and in walked the man he had already begun to dislike intensely: Charles Burke, the driving force behind Brandling Leisure Pursuits.

There was a little consolation in the apparent fact that Burke was in no way pleased to see Arnold. Burke was, however, a practised dissembler and he quickly cloaked both his feelings and his surprise. He softened the grimness of his mouth with a faint smile and he smoothed out the quick frown of recognition that had scarred his forehead, but he could not hide the sharpness of his glance; the eyes remained honest, at least, in their hostility.

'Mr Landon,' Charles Burke said flatly. 'I was expecting to see the Senior Planning Officer.'

'He went . . . out, some time ago. I'm expecting him back shortly but perhaps I can help you?'

Charles Burke hesitated, then extracted a cigarette case from the pocket of his tweed jacket and took out a cigarette. His lighter was gold, monogrammed; he waited until his cigarette was well lit before he replied. 'I wanted to have a chat with him, and I could wait for a while. It's about the planning enquiry, and when we're going to get some action.' He watched Arnold over the glowing tip of his cigarette. 'I don't imagine you'll be able to help.'

'The Senior Planning Officer did mention the enquiry to me,' Arnold said crisply, 'just before he went out. In fact, that's where he's gone—to make the necessary arrangements.'

'Arrangements?'

'For the next meeting. Colonel Summers wants it held at the Old Wheat Barn.'

For a moment he thought Charles Burke was about to lose his temper and explode into violent reaction. Then the heavily knitted brows relaxed, the mouth slackened, the square jaw became less belligerent in its jutting. Burke drew on his cigarette, in control again. 'The chairman of the committee,' he observed, 'seems to have a liking for the dramatic—or the ghoulish.'

Arnold was secretly inclined to agree but kept the secret to himself.

'I suppose,' Burke continued, 'it's an attempt to highlight this . . . er . . . discovery of yours, get it demonstrated in context. A good move, if he wants to rally support to his cause. But it won't work, Mr Landon.'

'I wouldn't wish to hazard a guess, Mr Burke.'

'Hmmm.' Burke hesitated, then glanced around at the meagrely furnished office. 'Do you mind if I sit down while I wait for the Senior Planning Officer?'

'Please do.'

Burke selected one of the two hard-backed chairs and sat down, then somewhat contemptuously regarded Arnold through the lazily climbing smoke spiral of his cigarette. 'They don't exactly go overboard to make you comfortable here, Mr Landon.'

'It serves.'

'Yes.' There was a silence, several minutes long, and

Arnold pretended to be busy with the papers in front of him as Charles Burke studied him with a disturbing intensity.

'Tell me, Mr Landon — what was it like, finding this . . . this secret joint of yours?'

The question took Arnold by surprise, and the surprise disarmed him to some extent. 'It was . . . exciting,' he blurted. 'That is . . . I mean . . .'

'You see, I don't quite twig you,' Burke said slowly, in a slightly puzzled, but amicable tone. 'You're a bit beyond my comprehension. All right, our backgrounds are obviously different — you're country-bred, I guess, while me, I was dragged up in the East End. Different kind of lifestyle, you'll agree. In the East End you meet all sorts, or think you do. But not your sort.'

'What is my sort, Mr Burke?' Arnold asked.

'That's it. I'm not sure. I can't understand this excitement you talk about. Can't understand why you have this . . . obsession about old places. I mean, they're no *use*, there's no mileage in it, you don't get anywhere with it.'

'A matter of opinion,' Arnold said, rather more warmly than he had intended.

'So put me right,' Burke insisted. 'What is the kick you get?'

'I don't know that you would understand,' Arnold said.

'Try me.'

'It's difficult to know where to start. It's knowing, and feeling, developing the sort of confidence, the belief that what lies under your fingers is to be trusted, because it's immutable, unchanging, the raw material of history. It's the excitement of knowing from all your past experience that you have a discovery under your fingers . . . it's a flowing together of all the accumulations of years of research and reading and feeling, of looking at what splendours men have created in buildings and a range of constructions — from pens to barns to country houses. It's

the *understanding* of what a master craftsman might
have felt, the sense of pride he experienced in creating
out of the living timber a piece of art, tiny perhaps, or
with the soaring span of a cathedral roof. It's this and . . .'
Arnold paused, aware that the excitement was catching
him by the throat, and recalling that he was speaking to a
philistine who would pull down the Old Wheat Barn for
commercial purposes. 'And . . . all sorts of things,' he
ended lamely.

Charles Burke looked at him with unmoved, appraising
eyes. 'But you work in a Planning Department. There
can't be much scope for this.'

Arnold shrugged. 'It gives me certain opportunities — like
the Old Wheat Barn. For that matter, what job *would*
give me the opportunities to undertake the kind of work I
enjoy so much?'

'An academic life?'

For a moment Arnold thought it was a goad, a reference
to Professor Fisher; he decided that was too subtle a
point, and if it was to be bait from Burke, he would rise to
it. 'The academic life,' he said warmly, 'produces the
wrong kind of environment for the kind of study that
fascinates me. It's too far divorced from reality. Many
academics, it seems to me, have almost a vested interest in
not knowing, in not discovering, because the truth, the
reality, would disturb their theoretical games. They don't
mind taking issue with the things I might propound, but
you saw Fisher's reaction, for instance — his insistence on
sources I would regard as secondary but which he had
already decided were of primary importance . . .' His
voice died away; he should not have mentioned Fisher.
But Burke appeared not to have noticed.

'So if not an academic life, what?'

'What indeed?' Arnold replied in a tone deliberately
flippant.

'I'm serious,' Charles Burke said, and from his eyes

rather than his tone Arnold believed he was.

'I'm happy enough as I am.'

'But there are constraints,' Charles Burke insisted. 'It's clear that if you're so . . . *enthusiastic* about the past, a job in the county planning department can hardly give you the opportunity to do your own thing.'

Arnold had not really thought about it, not sat down and consciously considered the situation. His background and his upbringing; the legacy his father had left him — far more valuable than money or property for it had been the bequest of intellectual stimulation; the whole driving passion of his adult life: all this had been an end in itself, but at the same time it had not been consciously measured against the demands of the need to earn a living. The Senior Planning Officer's drawing Arnold into the Planning Department had meant that Arnold was nearly placed to the objects of his interest: maybe the museum service would have been more appropriate, or even Parks and Gardens. Arnold had not thought about it: rather, there had been the escape from the dreadful drudgery of the Town Clerk's Department (although even that had taught him about secondary documentary sources such as leases and conveyances), and then the opportunity to look at maps and plans, on paper and on the ground. It had been close enough, affording him the chance to see buildings and situations he would not otherwise have come into contact with — but a better job, a more appropriate job? He had, quite simply not considered the question. And something told him now, perhaps he should not consider it.

'It simply occurs to me,' Charles Burke said slowly, 'that a man with your committed interests might well wish to look elsewhere, seek the kind of support that might enable him to develop his interest, for the benefit of the community at large, perhaps.' When Arnold remained silent, Burke went on, 'You see, let's take Professor

Fisher. There are those in the academic world who sneered at Fisher, because they denigrated his . . . marketing methods. He sold himself, he sold his interests, but why did he do it? Because he wanted the chance, the support, the financial base which would enable him to push back the—what is it called?—the frontiers of knowledge. Less energetic men derided him as a TV pundit; criticized him for his *projection*, his development of a cult figure, an image. But what they failed to see was the *objective*—and that objective was an academic one. Professor Fisher was *using* the system—and to effect, I might add.'

'I'm sorry, Mr Burke, I don't see—'

'Hear me out. Fisher knew what he was about. But you, Mr Landon, you're an innocent abroad. You do your thing, true, but on a shoestring. Fisher, now, he milked the system, got support, and used it for his own purposes. He was a *realist*.'

'The application to my own situation—' Arnold began slowly.

Burke raised a hand, silencing him. 'Let's take cases,' he said. 'Fisher had a point of view. He was prepared to hold to that view, come hell or high water. But also, if he could get financial backing *and* stick to his point of view . . . well, where's the harm in that? And that's what he was about.'

Arnold was beginning to see the light. 'You mean his argument about the Old Wheat Barn—'

'Was sincerely held. But there was nothing wrong in capitalizing upon that viewpoint. In obtaining financial support because of the force with which he could make that point of view.'

'Financial support . . . from Brandling Leisure Pursuits?'

Burke made no reply. He stared at Arnold fixedly. After a little while Arnold said, 'There's one problem in that kind of situation.'

'Tell me.'

'It leads to compromise.'

'We all have to compromise at some time or other.'

'Not on matters of principle.'

'Such as—?'

'Such as the age of the Old Wheat Barn,' Arnold said distinctly. He waited in the gathering silence, and then added, 'As I believe Professor Fisher might have compromised.'

'You'll have to spell that out,' Charles Burke said calmly.

Arnold shrugged. 'I can't be sure. It's a feeling you get . . . a gut feeling. I'm quite prepared to believe that Professor Fisher really was convinced that the barn was a sixteenth-century structure. But during the last hearing of the Planning Committee I think some doubts crept in.'

'On what evidence—'

'I told you,' Arnold cut in. 'Just a feeling. But let's take a case. Assume a man—an academic who is committed to the pursuit of truth and who believes in academic rigour and honesty, but who pursues that course by, as you put it, milking the system—let us assume that man holds a belief, but it is then shaken, or even just open to question. What should he do? Question his belief . . . put it to the test. But what if there are other considerations . . . *financial* considerations to be taken into account?'

'He'd be a fool to ignore them,' Burke said drily.

'But in ignoring them, he is in danger of allowing his academic judgment to become clouded. He loses the capacity to distinguish; he loses his vision of the truth.'

There was something thudding in Arnold's veins; he felt a mounting excitement that held a hint of danger, a fever, the sharpness of a knife edge along a jugular vein. A movement, and the blood could flow.

Burke inspected the end of his cigarette. Quietly he said, 'I have no academic background. I never could understand arguments that were stated in velvet phrases.

Vision; truth; academic integrity: they're matters beyond me. I need to be given clear statements.'

'Then I'll be clear,' Arnold said, breathlessly. 'I think you almost made a mistake. You thought I was like Professor Fisher.'

'And what was Professor Fisher like?'

'He had lost his way. As you say, he had started using the system, and was doing it well, was proud of his ability to use it. But in that committee room, I saw his eyes, and I think I know now what I saw in them. It was a realization that he had walked down a path that was dangerous.'

'I'm afraid, Mr Landon, I have little idea what you're talking about,' Burke said, but his eyes held a hint of sharp hostility.

'Professor Fisher was a disturbed man in that committee room. He had sold his academic soul—to you. That was all right, just as long as he believed in the viewpoint he was pressing. But I suspect he was beginning to have doubts . . . and those doubts should have dictated a fresh, unbiased look at the facts. But how could he do that when he was about to receive a sum of money to press his case?'

'From whom?'

'From Brandling Leisure Pursuits.'

'I see.' Smoke trailed lazily around Burke's grim mouth and eyes. 'So . . . ?'

'So Professor Fisher was disturbed; he saw his academic integrity ebbing away. Worried, concerned, he felt that he had sold his beliefs for . . . for . . .'

'Go on.'

Arnold hesitated. He stared at the cool Charles Burke and there was a fluttering in his chest as vague, half-formed notions jostled for position in his mind. 'I understand you . . . you and Professor Fisher fell out after the planning meeting. There was a . . . disagreement.'

'Was there, indeed?' Burke said softly.

'It would have been about Fisher's support of your application, albeit indirectly; Fisher would have told you he could no longer be as firm in his opposition to my theory about the Old Wheat Barn. And you would have replied that if he did not persist in his firm opposition to my dating—and hence the listing of the barn as a protected building—you would withdraw whatever financial support you had promised his university department.'

'Somehow,' Charles Burke said, 'we seem to have gone around in a circle. I'm not at all sure where this conversation is leading us.'

The fluttering had turned to a hammering that made it difficult for Arnold to speak. 'I . . . I think you were about to make me an offer, a little while ago.'

'My dear man—'

'No, I think you were going to make me an offer. That talk about how I might feel constraints in my job . . . I think you were going to say that it could be avoided if *you* offered me a job, or money, or support—'

'But why should I do that?' Burke asked lazily, but there was an edge in his tone.

'Because there would be a price tag,' Arnold replied. 'I would have had to promise to forget about the Old Wheat Barn.' There was a short silence during which Burke observed Arnold with a sardonic smile. At last, tense as a bowstring, Arnold blurted out, 'Isn't it the truth?'

Burke shook his head. 'And if I *had* made such an offer?'

'I would have rejected it,' Arnold said fiercely. 'As I think Fisher rejected it, when he came to his senses.'

Charles Burke yawned, stubbed out his cigarette, glanced at his watch and rose to his feet like a cat stretching supple, powerful muscles. 'I really can't wait any longer for the Senior Planning Officer . . . or waste time talking to his subordinate. But . . . I've made you no offer, Mr Landon, let's be clear about that.'

'But you thought you had Fisher all sewn up,' Arnold insisted, 'and you quarrelled with him when he had second thoughts. That's why he drove out to the barn the night he died. That's why—'

Something glittered in Charles Burke's eyes, hard and cold as a sliver of ice. 'I've no idea why Fisher went out there, Mr Landon, and I suggest you consider carefully what you might be about to say. As for this talk about offers . . . and quarrels . . . I really think you'd better get back to your mediæval lap joints. I think you are safer on such ancient familiar ground.' He flicked his cigarette butt away contemptuously. 'And you'll be safer keeping other theories to yourself.'

But after he had gone the theories were still looming painfully large in Arnold's mind. Because he could remember the look of shame in Professor Fisher's eyes at the committee hearing; the Professor had begun to doubt his own judgment, was aware of the pressures of financial support from Burke and what it entailed. It had led to a need to disentangle himself from Burke's clutches; a quarrel; and it had led to the need to satisfy himself that he might yet be right. He was sure of his academic ground, his documentary proof, but Arnold's claims in the committee hearing had been of a kind unfamiliar to him. It would have been the reason for his visit to the Old Wheat Barn; he had wanted to be there among the dust of the past, in the darkness, wanting to *feel* as Arnold had felt; experience the emotional reaction that had led Arnold to climb among the lofty rafters. Uncertainty and anxiety and shame had led Fisher out to Rampton Farm . . . and his death.

And Charles Burke would have known that he had probably lost the academic support that could have overwhelmed, by its weight, the half-baked theories of a planning officer called Arnold Landon. The question was: if

Professor Fisher had changed his mind and thrown his weight behind Arnold Landon's theory about the Old Wheat Barn, how far would Charles Burke have gone to prevent it?

There would have been a great deal of money at stake; there still was; would not a man of Burke's background and popularly rumoured violent propensities, have taken steps to remedy the situation?

Could such steps have led to murder?

CHAPTER 5

1

The Senior Planning Officer was somewhat disgruntled and had lost his usual suavity when he returned from his visit to the police headquarters at Morpeth. 'Do you know,' he said to Arnold, 'they actually see no harm in the Planning Committee going out to Rampton Farm! I spoke to a man called Tudor: there's something devious about him, a typical Welshman, if you ask me. He said that since they had now completed a physical search of the premises and the fields for clues to the killer of Professor Fisher, there was no problem about our holding a meeting at the barn. No, he was almost dismissive about the whole thing. He seemed rather more interested in asking me questions about you. You've already seen him, haven't you?'

Arnold nodded. 'What . . . what kinds of questions did he ask about me, sir?'

The Senior Planning Officer was unable to avoid evasiveness marking his tone of voice. 'Oh,' he said, deliberately offhand, 'just general questions, really. A few that were designed to check on answers you'll already have given in your statement; the rest of it was just about you as a person. You know — whether you were given to fanciful, nervous reactions; whether you were anxious, a worrier; that sort of thing.'

'I suppose he also asked,' Arnold remarked with a trace of bitterness, 'whether or not I had ever displayed any tendencies towards violence.'

The Senior Planning Officer looked vaguely uncomfortable. 'He did ask, as a matter of fact. I told him the truth — that I had noted no such propensities.'

Hardly the kind of positive reply that would have strengthened Arnold's situation: the Senior Planning Officer could have laughed the whole idea out of court instead of saying he had 'noted no such propensities'. Arnold shook his head angrily. 'Chief Inspector Tudor would have been better employed talking to, or about, Charles Burke, it seems to me.'

The Senior Planning Officer was clearly alarmed at Arnold's vehemence; perhaps he considered it might be a prelude to the kind of reaction he had discussed with Chief Inspector Tudor. He took an involuntary step away from Arnold's desk. 'Burke? Why should you say that?'

'Mr Burke was in here a little while ago.'

'What did he want?'

Arnold shrugged. 'A discussion with you, sir, about the planning application. I imagine he'll have wanted the latest information on the state of play; or maybe it would have been something rather more sinister.'

The Senior Planning Officer elevated his eyebrows. 'Sinister? What *can* you mean?'

Arnold felt suddenly very tired. He ran his hand across his eyes, rubbing his eyelids. 'It's the Old Wheat Barn thing, sir. I think he'll have come in to see you to discover whether or not he couldn't persuade you to a certain course of action.'

'Which would be?'

'To make me withdraw, officially, my statements about the dating of the Old Wheat Barn.'

There was a short silence. The Senior Planning Officer regarded Arnold from below lowered brows. At last he said, 'I have never made a secret of my . . . ah . . . unhappiness that you saw fit to make the statements you did. But they were not made in a professional capacity: they were personal statements for which this office is not responsible. So there is no question of an official withdrawal. No *official* support has been given to the theory.'

Which was one reason why the Planning Committee was still at sixes and sevens, Arnold knew. Members would have consulted the Senior Planning Officer and received no assistance whatsoever. He was fence-sitting, uncommitted. *He* would describe the attitude as impartial.

The Senior Planning Officer cleared his throat. 'I wonder how Mr Burke would have sought to *persuade* me, as you put it.'

'I don't know, sir,' Arnold replied, but he could hazard a guess. So could the Senior Planning Officer, who began to finger the lapel of his elegant suit nervously. 'Did . . . did he make an appointment to come back to see me?'

'No, sir.' Arnold hesitated. 'I think he was . . . *satisfied* after a brief discussion with me.'

The Senior Planning Officer stared at Arnold for several seconds. 'Are you telling me—'

'No, sir, I didn't tell him I'd withdraw my claim. We spent more time talking about and around the problem, and about Professor Fisher. But I believe Mr Burke was left, finally, with the knowledge that I would persist in my claim.' Arnold paused. 'Whatever his attitude might be.'

The Senior Planning Officer glanced vaguely around the room as though he wished he were not there. All he had wanted was an uncluttered enquiry. 'This planning application . . . I have the proposed costings on my desk now. And the possible company turnover, together with the job opportunities that are claimed will arise in the area. There's a lot of money in it all, Arnold; and a lot of money to be made. And Mr Burke . . . his background . . .' He fixed Arnold with almost a plaintive air. 'Are you *sure* about this discovery of yours, Arnold, and is it really as important as you say?'

'I'm certain, sir,' Arnold affirmed, 'and believe me, it is.'

It was eleven o'clock when the Planning Committee convened at the committee room under the chairmanship of Colonel Summers and the first submission was made by Charles Burke's lawyer, Mr Farnum. He rose and addressed the chairman, with the explanation that the documents he was now placing before the committee were of two kinds. The first batch related to the planning application *per se* and included certain assurances that were specifically designed to answer some of the objections that had been raised to the plan within the committee. Thus, he stressed, certain contractual arrangements would be made for compensation for disturbance with regard to nearby and adjoining owners. The allocation of an area of land to the north side of the property would be stocked for rough shooting and would be made available on rental to local sportsmen. The new outline plans he placed before them attempted to answer some of the environmental objections that had been raised, notably through the planting of mature trees to screen part of the building activity. And, finally, the last schedule described further and in detail the benefits that the project would bring to the area as a whole in terms of employment prospects, not least in the Gilsland and Carlisle projects. 'And now, Mr Chairman, we may turn to the second set of papers I place before you.'

These, he explained, had been drawn from university,

local and archival material held in Northumberland,
Yorkshire and the British Museum. A perusal of this
documentation, supplied by and verified by the leading
experts in the universities and the Museum Service, would
demonstrate to the absolute satisfaction of every member
of the committee that the claims made by Mr Arnold
Landon with regard to the Old Wheat Barn could only be
described as spurious. The notes for the documentation
had been checked and verified by the aforementioned
experts, and they constituted a summary of the total case
which, in its effect, was destructive of that put forward by
Mr Landon.

Colonel Summers puffed out his cheeks and looked
warily at the documents before him. He cocked an eye in
Arnold's direction. 'Mr Landon?'

Arnold looked swiftly through the summary. He
nodded. 'Mr Farnum is quite correct in his observations.
This summary is quite destructive of my claims.'

Farnum tucked a thumb into his waistcoat and smiled
confidently at his client, Charles Burke. But Burke kept
his sharp, appraising glance fixed on Arnold Landon.

'Unfortunately,' Arnold said, 'I see nothing in these
papers which can be described as new. They constitute
nothing more than a reiteration by the academic world of
the views put forward by Professor Fisher.'

Farnum was annoyed. Unhooking his thumb and
jabbing at the air with it, he snapped, 'Do you deny that
the weight of academic opinion is against you?'

Arnold nodded. 'I do not deny it. I merely assert it is
wrong — for the reasons I have already placed before this
committee on the occasion of its last meeting.'

Colonel Summers sighed, with a hint of satisfaction. 'In
other words, we're back where we started. The decision
has been taken to allow the committee to inspect the barn
and obtain direct evidence, with their own eyes, of the
location of this . . . ah . . . joint that Mr Landon speaks

of. We now intend to implement that decision. This meeting,' he announced, 'will convene at the Old Wheat Barn at three o'clock this afternoon. The meeting stands adjourned.' He rose and left the room, trailing the members of his committee behind him.

Arnold gathered up his own papers and then glanced across the room. Charles Burke was still sitting there, with Fred Rampton standing beside him. They were both staring intently at Arnold and the message in their eyes was precisely the same.

Whatever doubts Arnold might have had earlier about Charles Burke and the ruthlessness of which he might be capable were not dissipated as he recognized the murderous hostility in Burke's eyes, and saw its echo in the glance of Fred Rampton.

The council members had arranged to have lunch at Morpeth before setting out on the journey across country to Rampton Farm, and several cars had been made available by the Senior Planning Officer for their transportation. He announced to Arnold that he would be travelling with the committee members but that there might be a little difficulty over the seating arrangements, so it might be as well if Arnold made his own way to the farm and the Old Wheat Barn.

Arnold agreed, and shortly before one o'clock he left Morpeth and began the cross-country drive that was now becoming unpleasantly familiar to him.

There was a heaviness in the air that made him wind down the window of the car. The sky was a mackerel colour, heavy with humidity, solid, unmoving cloud barriers lying across the countryside and bringing an unnatural hush to the air, a greying of the green fields, a silence among the breezeless hills. The trees stood stiffly under the silence and though far away to the west, where the cloud pall was darker, Arnold saw the pale flickering of lightning, he felt that it would be a storm that would drift away south and not bring an early relief to the afternoon. His head began to throb as he drove and he put it down to the heavy humidity of the day, but there was a suspicion in his mind that his physical state was also affected by the way Rampton and Burke had been looking at him.

They regarded him as an enemy; and one man, whom they had regarded as a supporter and who had, it seemed, begun to turn coat, now lay dead. It was fanciful, Arnold argued to himself, foolish and non-sequential as an argument, but nevertheless the perspiration was staining the neck of his shirt, there was an unpleasant clamminess under his armpits and his mouth was dry, his tongue seeming to be swollen against the rasp of his teeth.

He had not felt hungry that morning, and he had made no arrangements for lunch. He was not hungry now, but he did need a drink. He glanced at his watch and calculated that within twenty minutes he would be passing the George Hotel, so he could stop there, have a drink and while away some of the time until the committee members arrived at Rampton Farm.

For not only would he be able to slake his thirst; he would be among company. He did not face the prospect of being alone in the vicinity of Rampton Farm with any degree of equanimity.

His timing was accurate. He arrived at the George Hotel shortly before two o'clock. But the inn presented a quite different appearance from the occasion of his first visit: the car park was crowded and Arnold was forced to leave his car on the grass verge some distance from the hotel. He realized that the hotel must have been taken over by a wedding party; in such circumstances he would normally not have gone in, unwilling to find himself in such a large, noisy gathering of strangers. But his head still throbbed, and his thirst had increased: the thought of a glass of lager was an irresistible temptation.

Arnold walked into the lounge bar.

It was packed. A throng of men stood at the bar struggling to get attention: the barman was there, with the support of the waitress who had recognized Arnold and a buxom lady who was probably his wife. The three were trying to cope with the rush of orders and were sweating profusely: behind the three-deep crush at the bar groups of men and women stood talking and laughing, and in the far corner the bridegroom clutched his bride's hand. Both looked excited but bemused, and as Arnold stood there he saw the bridegroom steal a covert glance at his watch.

Arnold went into the other bar.

Most of the regulars had congregated there, and the situation was less frenetic. Arnold had to wait for some time to get served, but it was neither as hot nor as crowded; similarly, there were no shouted inanities about the married state to suffer.

Arnold obtained his lager, ordering a pint to avoid a second early trip to the bar, and then managed to find a seat in the corner, near the door. Two men in working clothes were seated to his left, absorbed in a game of dominoes: Arnold sipped his lager after the initial long swallow, and watched them play for a while.

Then he began to feel the same curious sensation he had experienced at the Planning Committee. Someone was watching him. The hairs prickled at the back of his neck and the perspiration turned cold on his body. He hardly dared move his head for fear he might catch sight of one of the Ramptons, or Charles Burke. He sipped his drink again but the sensation remained powerful and at last, unable to help himself, he turned his head and stared straight back into the eyes of the man seated beside the window.

For a few seconds he did not recognize the long, lugubrious features, the downturned mouth, the eyes that held hints of a lifelong dissatisfaction with the manner in which the world had treated him. Then, as the man nodded reluctantly in recognition, Arnold realized who it was: Jack Sorrell, the man who held a grudge against the Ramptons for some old quarrel over land and water rights and fencing, and who now worked for Ben Kelvin at Newman Farm.

Something almost clicked into place at the back of Arnold's mind at that moment, like a worn gear taking up its accustomed task only to slip away into inefficiency again. It was something to do with Jack Sorrell and Rampton Farm . . . or was it that? Arnold shrugged mentally: his head still throbbed and he really did not have the cerebral energy to pursue the matter, trivial as it probably was. He turned his attention away from Sorrell, indifferent to the man's continued stare, and again sipped his lager while his pulse rate, accelerated by the absurd fears that had touched him a few moments ago, returned to normal. The noise from the lounge bar was reaching a crescendo as a certain amount of horseplay seemed to occur. From the catcalling, it was apparent that the bridal couple were about to take their leave. One or two men in the public bar stood up by the window, staring out and laughing at the antics of someone outside who was making the traditional adjustments to the rear bumper of the wedding car.

Arnold leaned back in his seat and listened to the cacophony of sound as the guests swept out into the car park: horns blared, there was much shouting, and then at last as several cars roared away the shouting died, there was a banging of doors and people began to straggle back into the pub, greatly reduced in numbers and noisiness.

Most of the family would have gone now, only the committed drinkers and the bachelor groups remaining in the lounge bar. Arnold glanced at his watch: another half-hour to pass before he need leave for Rampton Farm. He still felt a considerable thirst, but one or two lagers was usually his limit: a third was stretching things a bit. Even so, half an hour . . .

Arnold rose and walked across to the bar. The buxom woman was sitting on a stool behind the bar, holding a gin and tonic. The waitress also had a drink, but was chatting to one of the male wedding guests whose intentions were clearly inclined towards consummation but not the preceding formality. The barman himself was standing beside her, his bloated pot-belly pressed against the bar as he raised a pint of brown ale and downed it with a regular, steady pour. Arnold waited patiently. He was in no hurry.

When the barman finished his drink he caught sight of Arnold. 'Hah, needed that, sir,' he said and came across towards Arnold. 'Weddings is thirsty business.'

'I'll have a half of lager, please,' Arnold said.

'Aye, thirsty business, but profitable. Locals, they often use the back room for a meal and then spill out into the bar here for the drinking. We get a real bump up in our takings on do's like this. There you are, sir.'

He accepted the pound note Arnold tendered and went across to the till for the change. 'Mind you,' he said, winking as he came back, 'only just in time, wasn't it?'

Arnold held out his hand for his money. 'How do you mean?' he asked innocently.

'Didn't you see her?' The barman laughed throatily. 'She's in the club or I don't know what's what!'

The buxom woman on the stool snorted and sipped her gin and tonic. 'Don't listen to him, mister,' she warned. 'He says that about every wedding that goes.'

The barman shook his head and rolls of flesh around his chin wobbled. 'Not true, and you know it. But I got an eye for the ones that are in the family way.'

'Rubbish,' the buxom woman said scornfully.

The barman turned away and, unwillingly, Arnold found himself being addressed in a confidential tone. The big man leaned over the bar and winked again. 'She don't like me talkin' about it, but facts is facts. There's somethin' about a pregnant woman, you know what I mean? I'm not talking about when they start to waddle, when they get to wearing those clothes that accommodate their size, all that sort of thing. I mean, not when it's *obvious*. No. I'm talking about *before* that. Before it begins to show . . . show to a woman, anyway.'

Arnold was slightly embarrassed and wished to move back to his seat; nevertheless, in spite of himself he was baffled by the male arrogance of the barman and curious as to what exactly he meant.

"I don't quite follow . . .'

'Hell, you know what I mean! A woman, now, she doesn't recognize what's happened in another woman, but a man does. *I* do. They're different, you know what I mean? When a young girl gets pregnant, she's a different kind of person. She holds herself different; there's a different, maybe a more confident set about her head. She walks different — damn, she even *talks* different! Maybe it's got something to do with her achievin' what she was built for — motherhood. I dunno, really. All I *do* know is I can spot 'em a mile off. And I tell you that lass in there today, she was already up the stick.'

The buxom woman materialized at the barman's elbow. 'You talk a lot of bull, you do.'

He laughed in her face. 'Think back, old girl. Didn't *I* tell you the twice you was pregnant? Before you could get it out to tell me?'

'That was different,' the woman hedged. 'We was married and —'

'Nothing different about it. I'm telling you, when a girl's pregnant she begins to glow; she plumps out and her skin gets clearer than it's ever been. She lights up like there's a lamp inside her, warm and glowin' and lovely. A kid is at her most beautiful when she's just started to carry. And I can *tell*. I never been wrong yet, and that'll be the day, old woman, when you can prove that I am!'

They were still half-wrangling about it when Arnold carried his drink back to his seat. In the meanwhile, Jack Sorrell had gone.

Arnold sat down. He felt vaguely uncomfortable, his mental processes mushy, his head still aching, and a certain tension spreading throughout his nervous system. Perhaps it was the unaccustomed intake of alcohol at lunchtime; perhaps it was the thought of the committee meeting at the Old Wheat Barn looming ahead of him. Or maybe it was the feeling that no man should look at another the way Fred Rampton and Charles Burke had looked at him.

Or was it in some way connected with Jack Sorrell? The last few days had been so confusing and now his confusion seemed total. Chief Inspector Tudor had hinted that Professor Fisher's death might lie in some way at Arnold's door and there was still the nagging doubt that Tudor might perhaps be right. But what had Fisher been doing at the barn? Had he really gone there to seek for himself the kinds of vibrations that Arnold had found there? Arnold had seen the self-doubt and the shame in Fisher's eyes at the hearing and he wanted to believe that the Professor had at least found his own integrity before the end. But was it worth losing life in the pursuit of integrity?

Arnold's mind still groped painfully with the question of why Fisher had died. Worms still crawled in his mind as he sought the answer, but they were in a struggling, enmeshed heap, indistinguishable, a confused mass. Charles Burke and James Rampton, Fred Rampton . . . there were motives and opportunities . . . but why did his mind return, always fleetingly, but return nevertheless to

Jack Sorrell? And to something the barman had said in that other bar.

Arnold sat on, sipping his lager, and the more he tried to concentrate, the more confused he got.

2

The Senior Planning Officer's nose twitched. It was a patrician nose, capable of expressing professional disdain, a searching nose that could display a discreet twitch of displeasure when guilty secrets were revealed, a haughty feature in a face expressive of indignation when the bounds of duty were crossed and personal pleasures allowed to interfere with the proper discharge of professional duties.

'Arnold,' he whispered, twitching, 'you've been drinking!'

Arnold coughed, shielding his mouth with his hand, discreetly. 'Not to excess, I assure you, sir.'

The expression on the Senior Planning Officer's face made it clear that *any* intake of alcohol during the middle of the day and before a planning meeting was a matter of excess and consequent castigation.

But, surprisingly, Arnold felt he didn't care. He was not at ease, and there was still a faint throbbing in his temples, a certain inexplicable light-headedness in his attitude, but as far as the Senior Planning Officer's views were concerned, Arnold did not at this moment care very much.

A small group of people had assembled at the gateway by the road: the cars were pulled up on the verge and Colonel Summers was marshalling his committee with all the enthusiasm of a retired war veteran who was reliving the dreams, rather than the reality, of the past. Arnold guessed the Colonel would want them to march in order across the field, in the full battle pack of their plans, documentary evidence supplied by Mr Farnum, and other irrelevant papers. Because it all *was* irrelevant in Arnold's view: the only really important issue was what lay under his hands that day, up among the rafters.

'Here come the Ramptons,' the Senior Planning Officer muttered, withdrawing his attention from Arnold's alcoholic peccadilloes. Arnold looked down towards the farm: Fred and James Rampton were making their way up the hill, having parked their own vehicle in the yard of Rampton Farm. Arnold turned his head to glance back to the group now marching, as Arnold had predicted, under Colonel Summers's direction: he could make out Charles Burke and Mr Farnum, the solicitor, at the back of the group. So Burke had not deigned to use the parking facilities at Rampton Farm: but then, he would have little in common with the Ramptons, other than greed and a commitment to the destruction of the Old Wheat Barn.

Arnold turned to the Senior Planning Officer. 'It looks as though there's likely to be quite a crowd.'

'Humph,' the Senior Planning Officer replied. He often humphed when he wished to express displeasure without commitment. Arnold scrutinized the second wave of the advancing army. Behind Charles Burke were the straggling numbers of those concerned with the public interest: the hangers-on, the vaguely committed, Ben and Alison Kelvin to the fore, a few faces he recognized from the hearings without being able to put names to them . . . and among them the discontented features of Jack Sorrell.

The Senior Planning Officer glanced up to the leaden, heavy sky. 'I think we'll have to get everyone inside the barn,' he pronounced.

'It won't rain till this evening,' Arnold predicted.

'Nevertheless,' the Senior Planning Officer said cryptically, and walked forward to greet the Chairman of the

Planning Committee as he drew near the barn.

There was a hushed, reserved air among the members of the committee. Little Mr Nicholas was no longer fussing; he cast covert glances around the area in front of the barn as though awaiting the *frisson* that Mrs Oldroyd was already experiencing: she was keeping close to Colonel Summers, clearly anticipating the need for his gallantry at some point in the proceedings. Even Peter Fenton was subdued: the brash butcher's son and supporter of Charles Burke was somewhat unnerved at being on the location of a murder enquiry. He had not expected local government committee work to lead him into this kind of situation.

They gathered at the entry to the barn in a hushed, expectant group, and the others shuffled into place behind them, like a silent, crescent moon of inquisitive humanity. Colonel Summers was having a muffled conversation with the Senior Planning Officer, nodding sagely, his white hair fluffing out damply under the humidity and the perspiration of the walk across the fields.

'All right, everyone,' Colonel Summers called out, turning to the crowd. 'The thing to do is to go into the barn — committee members first, if you please, and members of the public at the back.'

He led the way. They shuffled in, staring about them as though expecting to see a Leonardo da Vinci and disappointed at discovering only dim light, the dank odour of rotting leather and wood, an earthen floor littered with rubbish, and the tall, gloomy, cavernous reaches of the roof above their heads. Arnold stood in front of the assembly, beside the Senior Planning Officer.

'Well, Mr Landon, it's your show,' Colonel Summers said in his best imitation of Monty.

Arnold froze. He looked around him at the expectant faces: Fenton, Mrs Oldroyd, Nicholas, Colonel Summers and the rest of the Planning Committee, and there should have been a sign of encouragement from the Senior Planning Officer, a graceful inclination of his head, a brief smile, a movement of his elegant wrist, something. Nothing. The Senior Planning Officer was maintaining a completely impartial role in this matter. All he had ever wanted was an uncluttered enquiry. Arnold's tongue clove to the roof of his mouth in the best traditional manner.

Until someone spoke, to break the agonized silence. 'Perhaps,' Charles Burke said mockingly, but with an edge of dislike, 'Mr Landon has changed his mind.'

Warmth flowed into Arnold's veins again: he stared directly at Charles Burke and he shook his head. 'No, I have had no change of mind. It was here, in the Old Wheat Barn that I experienced one of the most exciting moments of my life.' And Arnold began to explain to them, tell them all what it had been like. And in moments it was as though they were not really there. It was as though he had no audience, as he spoke of how he had been first drawn to an appreciation of the touch and taste, the feel and warmth of the materials with which his father had worked. He described to them the sawdust in his father's workshop, the way its finest particles hung in the air like drifting gold, or clung to the hairs on his father's muscular forearms as he worked through the long, warm afternoons. Arnold told them all about his childhood and the woods, where his father had pointed out to him the young trees spurting out of the undergrowth in a struggle for survival, and the soaring beechwoods, the pines and firs that would one day, when matured, form the raw materials for much of his father's craft.

Somehow he was talking to them of a lost world, of the agricultural depression of the 'thirties, when his father was out of work but with time on his hands now to

develop his son's mind and understanding: the silence of
the hills they tramped, the villages nestling quietly in the
dales, the timber baulks that served as bridges over tiny
streams, black and hardened by the weather until they
were like iron. Decaying farm machinery littered their
path, and he visualized for them how a hundred-year-old
farm cart, rotting in a dark corner of a deserted farm-
yard, could produce under his father's eye and tongue a
landscape of village life that was peopled with
individuals, all together forming a community, a close-
ness and dependence one upon another, that had somehow been lost in modern times.

And he talked to them of his own searches into the past
when he was left only with the legacy of his father's voice
and teachings, when the man himself had gone. He spoke
of his visits to the soaring cathedrals, his investigations of
musty, dusty corners, his seeking out with sensitive fingertips the evidence of the ages. His father had given him the
basis: a profound knowledge of wood and the way it was
shaped and used by carpenters. To that he had added
over the years his own insights, his own developing skills
and what perhaps was the most important thing of all — a
feeling, a flair, a sensitivity to atmosphere. The kind of
sensitivity that had led him deep into the history of this
barn, had enabled him to reach back through the
centuries and hear the voice of a man long dead, through
the agency of the timber that man had worked and
caressed with hand and cutting tools, until he had formed
the perfection that was that man's trademark.

'For you must be perfectly clear about what I am
saying,' Arnold announced. 'That joint — the secret
nocked lap joint of John of Wetherby — is unique. It was
copied by no other carpenter: it was the perfected joint of
a man who had spent all his life working towards one such
perfection. Other men did equally good work, other men
displayed equal and better craft in the working of wood

for specific purposes. Many of them developed their own perfections. But this one belonged to John of Wetherby. And the other examples lie scattered in Yorkshire, at the abbeys, in the churches.' Arnold paused, drew a shuddering, emotional breath. 'That is why I consider this discovery is of such vital importance. Not because it was I who discovered it—that is totally irrelevant. The importance lies in the fact that it is the only example of such a joint in the north-east of England; the only example of *any* of his joints in a building so humble. It raises a myriad of questions for the devoted scholar, relating to why John of Wetherby might have worked on this barn, what was the history of the structure itself, what may account for the missing documentation in the archives which seem to lack any reference to the barn before the sixteenth century—a whole range of questions and issues that spring from the existence of this work of this ancient carpenter in the Old Wheat Barn. It cannot be destroyed; it *must* not be destroyed. The work itself is a priceless heritage; and that means the Old Wheat Barn itself is something that can never be replaced in the county. To destroy it in favour of a leisure complex would verge on the sacrilegious; to complete the plans on this planning application would be tantamount to criminality.'

And then suddenly, as he realized how fluently and at what length he had spoken, Arnold was speechless.

The Senior Planning Officer was staring at him; his mouth was slightly open, his eyes held a glazed look in them, not disapproval, but incomprehension. Arnold was puzzled. The Senior Planning Officer knew about Arnold's interests, and passions. Why should he be surprised?

Arnold looked around at the rest of the silent group in the barn. Almost to an individual, they had the same kind of rapt, committed attention in their faces—they lacked the incomprehension of the Senior Planning

Officer but it was replaced with something else. Awe.

The silence grew around them all, almost painful in its intensity, and then there was a slight shuffling at the front of the throng. Mrs Oldroyd moved forward, losing her nervousness, casting aside her inclinations towards self-effacement. She had been crying again, Arnold noted with amazement; crying because of his words.

'Mr Landon,' she said, almost whispering the words, 'where . . . where did you find it?'

Arnold decided to show them.

It was the drink, of course: he realized it later. It accounted for his light-headedness, for his exposing himself and his history, his innermost thoughts, his commitments, his memories of his father, all those things that a man best keeps buried in his heart and in his mind for fear of the ridicule that the world might heap upon him for his sentimentality. The alcohol had given him recklessness and candour; it had given him freedom from inhibition; it had endowed him with fluency, the ability to say what he really felt.

And when Mrs Oldroyd asked him to show them where he had discovered the secret nocked lap joint, it had been the alcohol which had given him the nerve to make such a fool of himself, climbing into the rafters like a schoolboy after birds' eggs, seeking to demonstrate the prize, to shout to the world his prowess.

But once he was up there, it was different.

Not to begin with. Arnold felt that he almost swarmed up over the roof timbers, but that was probably the alcohol reacting again. He perched up there in the darkness and he proceeded with an extension of his lecture. To the upturned faces below him he sketched in his own, partly fanciful history of the barn. He suggested it might have been built by a local farmer who was friendly with John of Wetherby, or who might have known the father of the girl John married at Hexham Church, prior to the carpenter moving south. He would have known of John's prowess, prevailed upon him to do this job and construct the finest barn in the north-east of England with his peculiar skills.

And John would have built these roof timbers, these long, curving, rib-like structures with green wood, carving the joints, locking them into place until they were hardly visible, and then as the green wood dried and settled and hardened, slotting them into place in the roof of the barn, his gesture of goodbye to the north he would never visit again.

And after John's death at Wetherby in 1370 there was only the memory of his work until that too faded and died. Thereafter, as the barn slumbered on through the centuries people went about their business, the race of master-carpenters was replaced by cost-conscious builders, the era of new materials, new priorities and new compromises was ushered in and the old skills disappeared with the old ways of life.

Except in individuals, men and women who were out of phase, unlinked with and uncorrupted by their times; men and women who looked back and breathed the air that their predecessors had breathed. People like Arnold Landon.

As he spoke, the silence below Arnold was absolute; his murmuring voice drifted through the barn with an almost dreamlike quality. The listeners did not need to strain for his words — Arnold knew they *felt* them, were aware of their import as they fell from the darkened rafters above their heads. They were the stuff of eternal truths, those words, and as such they were clutched by the listeners. Arnold half-lay, stretched along a rafter beam, his clothes dusty and begrimed, his fingers caressing the ancient wood that had been carved by John of Wetherby, feeling the shape and texture of it, visualizing the joint itself, and perched high above these others he felt a swelling of the heart, an invincibility in his veins that told him he was powerful, omnipotent, invincible. His words were undeniably truth; he had won their hearts and minds; the barn would not be destroyed but would remain as a monument to the craft of John of Wetherby, and he, the unconsidered Arnold Landon, would have triumphed over the academic might of the English universities.

And then, subtly at first, it began to change. A fuzziness descended upon him, a weakness of vision that caused the first tremors of nervousness, of realization of what he was doing. He became aware of his surroundings, not of their texture and history and romance and age, but of their height from the ground, and their general insecurity. He looked down and the faces below him became a blur that seemed to fade and then grow again in intensity. Then, as his confidence ebbed and the last euphoric mists of alcohol drifted away from his brain, he saw the faces below him with an awful, hateful clarity. They were all there, staring up at him, mouths open, watching, listening: the Senior Planning Officer and Colonel Summers, Ben Kelvin and his wife Alison and Charles Burke and his solicitor, Farnum. Fussy Mr Nicholson was there, and Mrs Oldroyd, still tearful; Peter Fenton was standing at the back of the group and at one side of the throng stood James Rampton and his uncle Fred, while on the far side stood the discontented figure of Jack Sorrell, alone even in this crowd.

Arnold was above them, under the roof, looking down as though he were a god in charge of their destinies and he saw their faces and read anxiety and greed, anger and excitement, concern and emotion in their eyes. And his mind began to veer again, confusions creeping in; he stared around at all those faces, and scraps of conversation came back to him.

It was then that his stomach finally revolted, at the

tension, the alcohol, the height and the sudden fear. Arnold vomited. As he roared down at them they scattered, squealing: he saw the panicked disapproval in the face of the Senior Planning Officer, and the terror in the eyes of Colonel Summers who had never had to face such an attack on the Western Front. They ran for the corners of the barn, and then for the grey daylight outside, and the sound of their amazed, distressed, annoyed, infuriated voices came washing back into the barn like the distant thunder of a winter sea.

But gradually it faded; there was no one left in the barn. Arnold remained where he was, lying along the rafter beam. After a little while, the Senior Planning Officer came in and peered up at him. 'Arnold? Are you all right? I must say . . . such a performance . . . won't have done your case any good . . . but Mrs Oldroyd, she thought I ought to come in to see if you needed assistance . . .'

Poor Mrs Oldroyd. Weakly, Arnold called down, 'No, I'm quite all right now, sir. Please tell her not to worry. I'll make my own way down . . . and back to Morpeth. Please don't wait.'

'Humph. Yes. Well, the committee is now dispersing. It's heard — and seen — quite enough. I'll . . . er . . . I'll expect to see you in the morning, Arnold.'

He walked out quickly, without waiting for an answer.

The silence swept back into the barn, and Arnold closed his eyes. He would stay here for a while and then he would need to get back to his car, drive down to the George, talk again to the barman. Confirmation.

He wanted confirmation of a suspicion that had lain at the back of his mind. He wanted confirmation for his own purposes, to relieve himself of his own guilt. But more than that, he wanted to understand.

For just as he had looked across in the committee room and seen what lay in the eyes of Professor Fisher, so, playing God, Arnold had looked down into the barn this afternoon, seen all those faces, all those eyes.

And one face, one pair of eyes that had locked with his, looked backward to the past and displayed fear and loathing, and shame.

And now Arnold needed to know. And in a little while, after he had rested, recovered from the pain in his chest and in his mind, he would climb down and make his enquiries, and then he would know.

He would learn why Professor Fisher had died in the Old Wheat Barn.

3

The sky had darkened, and the distant flashes of lightning that Arnold had seen moving south had now been replaced with a heavy, western blackness that seemed to spread like a suffocating blanket across the darkening hills. Arnold had flicked on the headlights of his car as he came up the road, and he had left the sidelights on as he parked it and made his way across the field to the Old Wheat Barn.

The barn was outlined against the deep dark green of the woods on the hilltop and Arnold recalled the morning when he had found the body of Professor Fisher: he had sensed that someone was up there watching him. It could have been possible. Soon, he might find out.

He looked about him at the gathering clouds. There would be no thunderstorm but the rain was on its way and with it would come some release from the suffocating humidity that had oppressed the county all day. The barman in the George had reckoned it had lost him a few pounds, what with the wedding as well. Arnold had not told him about his own, shameful, distressing loss: the culmination of various factors, but a final rejection of the alcohol, voiding the contents of a stomach rendered vulnerable by nausea and lack of solid food.

Arnold stood in the entry of the Old Wheat Barn. He turned and looked down across the fields. Lights gleamed in the windows of Rampton Farm; likewise, Alison Kelvin had turned on the kitchen lights against the darkening sky in Newman Farm, across the lane. The hill was quiet, the cars had gone and when the rain came it would blot out the hill and the trees and the Old Wheat Barn in a curtain of grey.

Arnold went into the barn.

It was dark in there now. Somewhere up among the tall rafters birds cheeped, but as he stood there they became silent, as though wary of his presence. He heard a brief scuttling sound in the darkness of the corner — a rat, perhaps, burrowing among the debris of years. Then the barn fell silent, waiting for the rain.

Arnold waited too. He was nervous, his fingertips tingling and his heart moving erratically in his chest, but his brain was sharp now, not misted with the memories of the years; his analytical faculties had returned, his mental processes had become less trammelled by the clouding fumes of alcohol, and he knew where he was going, why he was here, what he was waiting for.

He felt certain it was only a matter of time, of waiting. In a little while the rain started. It came first as the light drifting mist of spray in the doorway, then developed into the thin sound of tapping on the roof. Arnold went to the doorway and felt the moisture touch his face; there was a coolness in the air, the lifting of the heaviness of the day, and the sky above was almost dark now as the streaming curtain of rain drew its veil across the hill and the rain fell more heavily, the tapping turning to a heavy, patterned drumming.

Arnold moved back into the recesses of the barn. He found a baulk of timber, decayed at its edge. He sat

down, running his fingers over its surface almost automatically, but his mind was not attuned to his fingers. It
was fixed on what the barman had said, today and
earlier, and Arnold's mind drifted back to other times,
other days, as though he were in a different time again,
and dreaming.

And then he knew he was no longer alone.

The rain increased in intensity and the opening of the
barn was only faintly distinguishable against the general
darkness, a grey oblong slightly lighter than the background darkness. Arnold could make out little of the man
standing there, framed in the doorway. He wore a heavy
raincoat, its collar turned up against the driving rain and
the hat was settled firmly on his head; an old hat, its brim
sodden and dripping, protecting the back of his neck,
protecting the eyes that Arnold had seen when he looked
down earlier, from the rafters.

'I thought you would come,' Arnold said quietly.

'The car in the lane,' the man in the raincoat said.
'And you have been up here for a while. I wondered . . .'

'No. I think you *knew*,' Arnold interrupted.

The man in the raincoat was silent for a while. As the
seconds ticked past and the rain dripped from his hat and
shoulders to the floor he stood staring in Arnold's
direction, seeing very little but knowing it was Arnold
who sat there. At last he sighed, stepped sideways into the
protection of the warm darkness of the barn, and his
figure was almost lost to view. 'I thought you had gone,
after the others left,' he said at last.

'Only down to the village. To the George.'

'The George? Why there?'

'To get some information . . . or confirmation is a
better word. Of what I have heard, and, maybe, of what I
saw in your eyes.'

'Why have you come back up here? What do you want?'
There was a fierce, agonized intensity in the man's voice

but it was directed as much against himself as against Arnold.

'What do I want?' Arnold asked in a vague surprise. 'I suppose . . . the end of the story.'

'You're not very explicit, Mr Landon.'

Arnold managed a laugh. 'I've already done more talking than I should have done today—but that was alcohol. I'm sober now; and I think you know what I mean.'

The man shifted uneasily. The habits of years were with him still; the suppression of truth and the need for it lingered, controlling, defensive. He took off his hat, struck it against the wall violently, as much to vent his insecure anger as to shake away the rain that soaked it. 'I ask again, Landon. What do you want up here in the Old Wheat Barn?'

'I want to find out why Professor Fisher died.'

'That's a matter for the police,' the man replied shortly.

'But for me, too,' Arnold said. 'For, in a sense, I bear some of the responsibility. I feel that if I hadn't discovered that lap joint above our heads the Professor would not have died. It leaves me with a sense of involvement; a sense of guilt. It's a burden I don't want to bear for the rest of my life. But you must understand that. You know about the burden of guilt.'

'I—'

'I saw it in your eyes,' Arnold said simply. 'As I saw the shame in Professor Fisher's.'

The man was silent. Somewhere in the darkness behind Arnold there was a rustling again as the rat moved, creeping to a warmer, darker haven in the depths of the barn.

'You're a perceptive man, Mr Landon. You proved that today—perceptive, emotional, a *feeling* man. But I think all this you're hinting at, it has no basis in reality.

To talk of what you see in someone's eyes—'

'Windows to the soul.'

The man laughed, a short bitter sound. 'Poetry!'

'Reality.'

'What the hell do you know of reality, Landon? You're a dreamer, a man who is rooted in a dreamlike past! I heard you today, heard you talk and, yes, it was spell-binding. But that was because you were talking of a world long since gone, if it ever existed. It was probably quite different from your memories: smellier, dirtier, less happy, *smaller*. Your words weren't about reality, but about a parcel of half-remembered emotions. It was more akin to mysticism than truth.'

'It's my truth,' Landon replied quietly. 'And we all have our own truths, don't we? Was that why Professor Fisher died?'

The man was silent for a little while. Then, quietly, he asked, 'Why did you go back to the George? What did they tell you there?'

Arnold hesitated. 'Enough to make me guess that the death of Professor Fisher was probably an accident.'

The man moved in the darkness and the faint greyness from the doorway was reflected on the wet raincoat. He seemed to sag against the ancient wall of the barn, needing support for a moment. His voice was more strained when he spoke again. 'Perhaps you'd better tell me what you know.'

'Not know. Guessed. I've been puzzled all along about two things: the reason why Professor Fisher was here; the reason why he was killed. I'll probably never know precisely why he came out to the Old Wheat Barn and so that shadow of guilt will remain with me. But I think it was all due to a crisis of conscience. The financial offer he had accepted on behalf of his university department was dependent upon his testifying, with force and all the academic bluster he could raise, against my theory. If he talked me down, exposed my arguments for emotional rubbish, and with all his documentary support insisted that the barn was a sixteenth-century structure, then he would get his money. But he was torn.'

The man in the raincoat raised his head. 'What do you mean—torn?'

Arnold made a deprecating gesture with his hand. 'Oh, I don't mean that he was convinced by my arguments. I mean, merely that the seeds of doubt were sown in his mind. It's even possible that he might have discounted those doubts, if it hadn't been for the money. As an academic, he felt he ought to argue the case with me, but honestly, try to investigate my claims properly. That would mean meeting me, at some point at least. But he couldn't do that, not if the money was to be gained. And in accepting that restriction he was muffling his academic judgment, clouding his clarity of investigative thought.'

'I still don't understand why he came out here.'

'I think he was disturbed, frustrated, had reached an intellectual *impasse*. He still believed he was right; but he was worried that he might be wrong, and might be acquiescing in the destruction of a building of historical importance. But he had received so little assistance from me—I had merely talked of educated hands, of feelings, of atmosphere. So I think that he was forced into his action. If *that* was what *I* went on, and it led me to discovery, what would it do for him? All academics are arrogant; his arrogance—and his self-doubt—forced him to the conclusion that he must visit the barn, stand here in the darkness, drink in its atmosphere, seek the ghost of his own conscience and the solution to his own personal dilemmas.' Arnold paused sadly. 'The unhappy thing about it is that I don't believe he would have found anything but a cold, dark barn. There was nothing in Professor Fisher that would have made the barn *live*. But I hope he never discovered that, before you killed him.'

There was a soft sound in the darkness, the gentle expulsion of pent-up breath. 'Why do you say that?'

'That you killed him? Why else would you be here to-night talking to me?'

'Your car in the lane—'

'No,' Arnold interrupted. 'Let me explain. The first time I went to the George, the barman said several things to me but one of them was a recounting of an incident at lunchtime that day. A quarrel in the bar, in which Jack Sorrell was involved.'

'I don't see—'

'The quarrel was preceded by remarks made by James Rampton. He said he intended coming up here after dark and firing the Old Wheat Barn. Sorrell heard those remarks. I thought nothing about that at the time—my own anxieties were about the barn itself. It's why I drove up here that evening, to make sure the barn was still intact. It's possible you saw me . . . maybe from the woods.'

There was a short silence. 'Go on.'

'For the same reason I came out to Rampton Farm in the morning, to warn James Rampton that he should not be so foolish as to take the law in his own hands and fire the barn. And then I walked up to the barn and found Fisher's body. Perhaps I should have put things together then, but I was shaken and confused and I ran down to Newman Farm and Alison Kelvin took me in . . . But later, the Sorrell thing bothered me.'

'And now you've reached certain conclusions,' the other man said softly.

'As I said. That you made a mistake, committed an error.' Arnold took a deep breath. 'I believe you were told about the quarrel in the pub and you were afraid that James Rampton might do just what he had threatened to do. So you came up here to forestall him, to prevent him destroying the Old Wheat Barn. You probably waited in the woods at first, while it was still light, and then when darkness fell you came down into the barn itself, hid in the shadows, where it was warmer and drier. Because it could be a long night's wait.'

'I—' The sound was choked off, and Arnold went on.

'Then, about midnight, you heard a car . . . or even two cars, because it was about that time that James Rampton was making his drunken way home. You kept back in the shadows, waiting. And at last your worst fears were realized. You heard a movement outside the barn. At midnight, it had to be James Rampton coming to carry out his threat. You stepped forward in a rage, you were blinded perhaps as he swung up the torch, shining it directly in your eyes, and you reached out, grabbed him by the arm, swung him violently against the door of the barn, because he was a younger man than you, deserved what he got, and then—'

'I had no idea it would be Professor Fisher,' the man in the raincoat said quietly. 'And it *was* an accident. I had no intention . . . But it makes no difference. There's nothing of consequence to connect me to this matter. How you came to stumble upon it—'

'Sorrell,' Arnold said. 'His presence at the pub. It would be a natural thing for him to do, to tell *you* about James and his threats.'

'There's no proof—'

'I'm not concerned about proof,' Arnold replied in a tired voice. 'Only about my own personal peace. And now, perhaps, yours.'

The man's voice had tightened. 'What do you mean about peace? Fisher's death was an accident—'

'I think it probably was,' Arnold agreed. 'But that was the other thing I wanted to know. You see, I still felt a sense of responsibility for his being there. But why did *you* have to be there? In other words, I needed to know whether there was another reason behind Professor

Fisher's death. That's why I went back to the George this evening.'

4

It had been early, so there was only one regular in the public bar, nursing a pint. Arnold had gone into the lounge bar, still littered somewhat after the wedding party's depredations at lunchtime. The buxom lady was behind the bar and Arnold had asked her if her husband was available. She had yelled out behind the bar and after a few minutes he had emerged, sleepily. He seemed vaguely alarmed when he recognized Arnold, as though he was afraid Arnold was going to claim he had been shortchanged at lunchtime. When Arnold assured him he merely wanted a brief conversation and a glass of shandy — the effects of the lager were still horrific in Arnold's mind — the man seemed relieved. At Arnold's request, he poured a generous measure of lemonade into the puddle of beer, took Arnold's money, and then said, 'Now what was it you was wanting to chat about, sir?'

'A couple of things,' Arnold said. 'I was in here the other day, and you were telling me about a quarrel that broke out, involving James Rampton.'

'Ahhh . . .' The barman furrowed his brow and considered. 'When he was talking about firing the Old Wheat Barn, you mean?'

'That's right. On that occasion Jack Sorrell was here —'

'Thass right.'

'And heard the threats?'

'Of course. They was shouting at each other.'

With that confirmation, and the creeping suspicions now moving in his brain, Arnold had gone on to his next question. 'When I was in the lounge bar I saw a young girl today — just got married.'

The barman glanced around half ruefully, and nodded.

'And afterwards,' Arnold continued, 'you said something about her.'

The barman grinned. 'That I reckon she was pregnant already. Thass right.'

Arnold hesitated. Then, plucking up courage, he asked, 'Do you remember Molly Stavely?'

The barman frowned heavily for a few moments and then his brow cleared. 'Oh, we was talking about her the other day. First time you came in . . . aye, I remember that.'

'You told me at the time,' Arnold said slowly, 'that she was a plump-looking girl; you said she looked well . . . and then, today, when you were talking about the youngster who had just got married, you used the same kind of words in describing her.'

'Did I?' The barman had not been able to follow the line of Arnold's enquiry: he seemed vaguely nonplussed and he glanced over his shoulder to his wife as though for assistance. 'I may well have done,' he offered cautiously. 'But—'

'I was merely wondering,' Arnold prompted with equal caution, 'whether you had a similar view about Molly Stavely's condition.'

The barman was still frowning, still puzzled. 'Views about her condition?'

Arnold swallowed hard. 'The last time you saw Molly Stavely,' he blurted out, 'was she . . . did you think she was pregnant?'

The barman stared at him as though he were demented, asking him to pass a comment about someone he had not seen for decades. Then the brow furrowed again as the man considered. He pursed his lips. 'Wasn't as sure then; younger, I was, didn't notice things the way you do when you're older. But, well, I *thought* it was a possibility at the time. And it was kind of confirmed after, wasn't it?'

'How do you mean?'

The barman leaned forward, elbows on the bar, confidently. 'Well, think about it. Land Girl like that, most of them was easy . . . I mean, away from the city, from home, fresh air, warm grass and all that. Natural, wasn't it? There she was up at Fred Rampton's farm with Old Mother Rampton running the roost. She goes away, she comes back, and then she's got just the kind of confidence, bloom, the kind of *bearing* I been talking about. Leastways, that's how I *remember* it, though maybe I wasn't so sure at the time. Hindsight, like. But what happens? First she's in here one day, happy, plump, glowing; next day there's a row up at the farm, Old Mother Rampton throws her out and she scarpers back to Coventry or God knows where, the old lady dies and Fred, he goes rampaging off first chance he gets, Coventry way, and goes again afterwards, couple of times. Whaffor? To find that Molly girl. So, obvious, innit?'

'What's obvious?'

The barman looked at him with scorn. 'Stands to reason. Fred was stuck on her. They ended up in some hayrick. She thought she'd end up with a farm: instead, when she tells the old woman she's pregnant, Old Mother Rampton throws her out neck and crop. And Fred's too bloody weak to do anything about it. I mean to say, any man worth his salt, in a situation like that, he'd have told the old woman to go to hell. But not Fred. He just kow-towed, knuckled under and let the old bitch have her own way. She was a right tartar, I know that, but Fred Rampton should have stood up to her.' The barman had picked up a glass and started polishing it vigorously. 'I suppose he was worried about the farm . . . but there was no one the old woman could have left it to. There was only him. He'd have got it anyway. But he caved in, and I think he's lived to regret it.'

'How do you mean?'

'I tell you, I'm a local lad, been around here all my life. Fred, he wasn't a bad bloke as a youngster; but once he got stuck on that girl, got her in the family way, then showed no guts in standing up to his old lady . . . well, I think he sort of lost something inside. Lost his girl and the kid she was carrying. Got the farm, yes, but never found Molly — and I think something inside him soured then. He was never the same after that, know what I mean? He got sour and grumpy, lost interest in the land. And there it is now, Rampton Farm, not worth much as a farm after twenty years of neglect. All that's left to him, innit — selling out, I mean? All because he let his mother treat him like he was a snotty-nosed kid instead of a growed man who'd just put a young kid up the stick.'

Arnold hesitated, considering his next question. 'All this was . . . local knowledge?'

The barman frowned, had the grace to look vaguely uncomfortable. 'Knowledge . . . gossip. I don't know. The wife and I — we hadn't been married long then — we talked about it a bit. Don't know as there was all that much chat about it; I mean, during the war people came and went, and that girl Molly Stavely, she was sort of forgot, you know? She never came back. And though everyone knew Fred Rampton was off looking for her, well, we didn't talk about it too much. It was his problem; he'd made a fool of himself, but not up to us to call him because of it. And once he stopped looking, well . . . Only reason I remember, really, is that she looked so plump and nice, and the wife was expecting at the time and . . . well, sometimes, things like that stick with you, you know? If that bloody silly fool Fred had played his cards right, everything could have been so different, don't you reckon?'

The rain increased in tempo, drumming heavily on the

roof of the Old Wheat Barn as Arnold finished talking,
relating what he had heard in the George. The man in
the shadows was huddled in his raincoat, silent, head
hunched between his shoulders. After a long silence he
raised his hand, waved his wet hat vaguely.

'It was a long time ago.'

'But the barn is still here,' Arnold said.

'What's that supposed to mean?'

'Merely that I think the barman at the George was near
the truth.'

'Near it?'

'He had most of the facts. But there was a flaw in the
interpretation of them.'

The silence grew around them again, a heavy silence
marked only by the thunder of the rainstorm. The man in
the raincoat moved uneasily, nervous as the rat scrabbling in
the darkness behind Arnold. 'How can people ever know
what happens—'

'They can only guess,' Arnold said quietly.

'And you've made some guesses?'

'I have. In an attempt to *know*. The barman at the
George had *his* answers, but they were based on facts as
he saw them. There are other viewpoints: they deal in the
same essential facts, with some additions. Other people
have a different view of what happened. A young woman,
for instance, who was in love. A young woman whose
family had died, and who had a farm to run but no one to
love her, marry her, run the farm with her. She saw the
man she wanted, but he was already committed to someone else. So, quite deliberately, she put a proposal to him.
She *bought* him; and he allowed himself to be bought.'

'So?' the man in the raincoat challenged harshly.

'So what happened, Mr Kelvin,' Arnold said, 'to the
unfortunate Molly Stavely?'

Ben Kelvin stood away from the wall of the barn and
took a threatening step forward towards Arnold. 'You're

the one theorizing around here; you're the one dredging up the past for God knows what reason. You're the one with the answers. You tell me, Mr Landon. You tell me!'

'I really don't know,' Arnold said. 'The facts . . . I can talk about them, and the viewpoints, but beyond that . . .'

'All right,' Ben Kelvin said, breathing harshly. 'What are the facts as you see them?'

'As I hear them,' Arnold corrected him gently. 'First, the barman tells me he thinks Molly Stavely was pregnant. Then she was thrown off the farm; then Fred Rampton sought her, never found her, and sank into a despondent unhappiness. Because, the barman thinks, he had got her pregnant, was in love with her, but had lost her through his own weakness in not standing against his mother. But . . .'

'Go on.'

'But the other viewpoint is one given to me by your wife. She told me that *you* and Molly were in love, but that when Alison Newman dangled the bait of the farm before you, you took that bait and the marriage it entailed and turned away from Molly Stavely. Immediately afterwards, she left.'

'So?'

'So Alison Kelvin, the newly married bride, then noted the way in which your thoughts still turned regularly towards Molly Stavely. How you used to moon in the window for years, looking up towards the Old Wheat Barn where you and Molly used to meet secretly, perhaps make love in the warm darkness all those years ago. She saw you staring, thinking, remembering. But she said nothing, because she had you and that was enough. She didn't know that Molly Stavely was pregnant before she left Rampton Farm. If she were told, she would have assumed, immediately, that it was you, not Fred Rampton who had fathered the child. Same facts, essentially, but her view of them is different. She sees the cause of your difficulties with Fred Rampton rooted in a rivalry forty years old. A rivalry in which you won the prize, threw it away, and Fred couldn't find it, to pick up the pieces.' For a little while Ben Kelvin was silent. Then, thickly, he said, 'I never wanted to prolong the quarrel with Fred Rampton. But he wouldn't even speak—'

'Maybe because he knew that you had made Molly pregnant, and that he hadn't had the courage to keep her on the farm, pregnant by another man. At least, not until it was too late.'

'What do you mean, too late?' Kelvin asked harshly.

'Too late for him to find her . . . in spite of his searching in Coventry. But then, I suspect you knew he would never find her in that town.'

Ben Kelvin raised his head. A trick of the light, a stray gleam in the darkness caught his eye, made it glitter coldly, madly. 'What are you trying to say?'

'I'm merely looking at the evidence,' Arnold said in a quiet voice. 'A third viewpoint, a different point of observation. You got that girl pregnant but threw her over in favour of Alison Newman; Molly left Rampton Farm; Fred never could find her thereafter. But maybe he was looking in the wrong place.'

'You—'

'Because there are other facts to be observed,' Arnold interrupted. 'You married Alison Newman deliberately, not out of love. Your head ruled your heart. You worked hard on the farm, used modern techniques, developed it into what it is today. Your wife was interested in other things, like the old part of the farmhouse, but you weren't: to you, over the years, it was only the modernization and efficiency of the farm that attracted you. So there are the anomalies.'

'I don't know what you're talking about,' Ben Kelvin said, but his tone had become strangely quiet.

'Then let me put the oddnesses to you, and perhaps you can explain them. A man who threw aside a girl who loved him can hardly be regarded as a sentimental man. Indeed, his behaviour towards his wife thereafter is affectionate, but probably not loving: he and she knew it was a bargain, a buying and selling. Yet, oddly, that same man stares out of the window, night after night over the years. Can he *really* be dreaming, seeking the ghost of a lost love?'

Ben Kelvin shuffled, but made no reply.

'And then,' Arnold continued, 'there's the matter of the planning application. This man, he's obsessed with making his farm sound and profitable, but uninterested in the past. The Old Wheat Barn can mean nothing to him . . . indeed, is he *really* so suddenly concerned about the environment? It's never bothered him before, but suddenly he's vociferous against the scheme put forward by Brandling Leisure Pursuits. Can it be spite against Fred Rampton? Hardly, because he's been largely indifferent to the long-running score. Then, if it's not really the environment, and not Fred Rampton, it must be concern for the barn itself. But why? You see, Mr Kelvin, I think you *were* concerned about the Old Wheat Barn. You heard from Jack Sorrell about James Rampton's threat to fire it and you came up here to stop any such action. You were doing my job — *guarding* the barn. And you attacked Professor Fisher thinking he was James Rampton. The killing was an accident — but why were you at the barn in the first place? Why such an interest? It can only be the same interest that drew you to the window, staring out in a reverie. But not sentiment, Mr Kelvin, not the loss of a love. Something else.'

'Such as?'

'Fear.'

Ben Kelvin's breathing rasped harshly in the darkness. He moved, stepping closer to Arnold. 'You said something about . . . about Fred Rampton looking for Molly Stavely . . .'

'In the wrong place. That's right,' Arnold said calmly. 'He shouldn't have gone to Coventry. I don't think Molly Stavely ever left Rampton Farm. I think she stayed right here—in, or near, the Old Wheat Barn.'

Ben Kelvin made a choking sound. 'You can't know—'

'No, I don't know,' Arnold said, 'But the facts . . . and then, this afternoon, here in the barn, when I was up there on the beam, trying to explain about John of Wetherby, I looked down and it was like playing at God, and they all stood there staring up at me, caught, entranced even—except you. Not you, because the barn meant, and could only ever mean, something else for you. A remembrance, but not of love; a recall of horror and fear and shame and guilt. The shadow of the burden of shame I saw in the eyes of Professor Fisher was there in your eyes today as you looked up to me, but it wasn't a mere shadow, it was naked and desperate. You wanted my story to be true, right, acceptable, but for your own reasons. You wanted the Old Wheat Barn to be saved from destruction—but for your own purposes. And I saw some of those purposes in your eyes, and it was then that I lost control of my stomach. No, I didn't know, but the anomalies spun in my brain, the facts slotted into place, and I had to go down to the barman at the George for the confirmations that would fix my suspicions.'

'And you knew,' Ben Kelvin said tiredly, 'that I would be watching from Newman Farm. and that when I saw your car I would have to come up here, to find out what you were doing here, why you had come back.'

'Yes. I knew that. I knew you would come.'

Ben Kelvin was shaking his head slowly, as though trying to erase painful memories from inside his skull. 'You knew that, but all the rest was guessing. You could never *know*—you could never know how it was.' He swore

suddenly, blasphemously. 'It wasn't like that, you see!
You talk of viewpoints, but what about mine? All right,
same facts, but it wasn't the roses thing you imagine!
Molly Stavely, she was a bad one. I was working at the
farm and she set her cap at me, we became lovers the first
months she was here. Then she went back to Coventry for
a while. Her family were all dead then, and when she
returned we took up again but it was different — she had
an eye for the main chance, and the main chance was
Fred. She teased him, tormented him, so he didn't know
where he was going. We still met up here, at the barn,
but it was Fred she was after, and she would have got
him, too, if Mrs Rampton hadn't caught them together
one afternoon in Molly's room. *She* summed up Molly
better than either Fred or I ever could, and she told her to
get packed and away. So Molly turned back to me. We
met up here . . .' Ben Kelvin shivered suddenly and
looked about him at the dark, vaulted roof of the barn. 'It
was warmer in those days, closer, and friendlier . . .'

But it would have been mood, and lovemaking and the
erosion of fear that would have changed it, Arnold knew.
'What happened?' he asked.

There was a long silence. Then Ben Kelvin sighed. 'I
had that week spoken to Alison. She offered me the farm;
it was out of the blue; all I could ever want or dream of.
And now Molly was coming to me, telling me she was
pregnant, demanding that I marry her. Second best,
sure, but Fred was no longer available, and she *was*
pregnant . . . I told her it was out of the question, said the
baby could be Fred's as much as mine, told her I was
going to get married. And she went almost crazy. Started
to scream at me, kicking, biting . . . I put my hands on
her shoulder to hold her off. Her language . . . And then
she was quiet, and I realized my hands were tight on her
throat.'

Kelvin turned away suddenly and walked towards the

door of the old barn. He stood there silhouetted in the faint light, looking down the hill towards Newman Farm, shrouded by the curtain of rain. 'I used to wake at nights, terrified, thinking of her up here. I used to stare, and the horror and the terror and the guilt would seize *me* by the throat, the way I'd seized her. Over the years it never changed . . . And then I heard Fred Rampton wanted to sell the farm to Charles Burke. I went to see the planning application. It called for the destruction of the Old Wheat Barn.'

'And Molly Stavely is here?' Arnold asked gently.

'They would have found her when their bulldozers moved in,' Ben Kelvin said and slowly turned to face Arnold.

The rain stopped just as though a tap had been turned off and an eerie silence swept through the night, finding its focal point in the sudden tension that had arisen in the barn. Arnold rose slowly, facing the man who had killed twice in the darkness of the barn. 'Mr Kelvin—'

'I've lived with this for so long,' Kelvin said. 'I've hidden it from Alison, from everyone . . . No one missed Molly Stavely, except Fred, and he would never have been happy with her. It's been hidden so long . . . it can't come out now. I can't let it.'

'There's no way you can stop it now,' Arnold said breathlessly.

'There's only you, Landon. Only you.'

Arnold's heart was thundering in his chest as the menace in the air grew about him, almost palpable. Kelvin took a step towards him, murmuring in a drugged, painful voice, 'There's only you . . .'

'No,' Arnold said. 'There's you . . . there's you as well.'

As Ben Kelvin stopped abruptly, Arnold hurried on. 'You've kept the knowledge and the guilt all these years but I saw it in your eyes. It was made worse by the killing of Professor Fisher, because however Molly Stavely might have contributed towards her own death, Professor Fisher was completely innocent. Molly's death was on your conscience; Professor Fisher's death must be an added torture. Could you really add mine to that burden you already carry?'

In a little while there was only the softness of the dark night outside, and Arnold was alone in the barn.

The Senior Planning Officer's language worsened as he came storming into Arnold's office. He was using words which Arnold was pleased to describe to himself, privately, as excretives rather than expletives. He plunged up and down the length of the room angrily, waving his arms and swearing. Then he came to a full stop, staring down at Arnold. 'I suppose you've heard the news?'

'What news, sir?'

'That blasted man, Chief Inspector Tudor. He's started digging with a squad of men up at the Old Wheat Barn! He told me the Planning Committee could go up there because they'd finished their investigations, and now they're up there digging! What are they looking for, Arnold, what the hell are they looking for?'

He glared at Arnold, but when no reply was forthcoming, he went on, 'And then there's a rumour buzzing around Morpeth that Mr Kelvin of Newman Farm went into police headquarters yesterday, and hasn't come out since. His wife went in today and came out crying, got driven away in a police car. What the hell is going on? It all makes things to complicated. It makes everything so . . . cluttered.'

'The . . . er . . . the Chairman of Planning called in while you were out, sir,' Arnold offered. 'Left you a note.' Arnold passed the envelope to the Senior Planning Officer who ripped it open impatiently, his brow still clouded with incomprehension. Then, magically, within seconds the thunder on his brow cleared, and he smiled.

'Good Lord, Arnold, he's cleared off back to London!'

'Who, sir?'

'Charles Burke. That fellow Farnum phoned in to say that the planning application is withdrawn. You remember that newspaper cutting Summers produced in the Enquiry?'

'About allegations of bribery in proposals to extend the airport at Carlisle?'

'That's it. Seems it was sent in by one of the people involved, on the thesis that if *he* goes down others should go down as well; he'd now been implicating our friend Burke. There *was* some fire behind the smoke, and Burke now thinks it expedient to beat a hasty retreat. He's leaving the Ramptons high and dry and Brandling Leisure Pursuits are wasting no more time on the Old Wheat Barn.' He glanced at Arnold suspiciously. 'If this had come out properly, sooner, there'd have been no need for all the fuss . . . and this digging thing . . .'

Arnold made no reply.

'Ah, well . . .' Some of the Senior Planning Officer's cool elegance made its return; he twitched at his cuff. 'No matter, at least things will calm down again now and the planning application is dead. As for the Old Wheat Barn . . . once the police have finished with it, whatever they're up to, well, maybe we'll have a . . . er . . . *proper* survey done of it.' He caught Arnold's glance and assured him hastily. 'Not that I mean your theory . . .'

He humphed uncomfortably as Arnold smiled. 'Perhaps Historic Houses Section, sir . . . ?'

'Yes, good idea. Mmmm. Could be a feather in the department's cap, really. Yes. MMMmmm. On the whole, Arnold, I am really rather pleased with the outcome; yes, on the whole very pleased with you.'

But Arnold could feel no pleasure. He thought of the man who sat in Morpeth Police Headquarters and the woman who had lived with him for almost forty years, not knowing of his crime and fear. He thought of the gathering of ghosts in the Old Wheat Barn: Kelvin's, Fisher's, the fearful memory of an old crime and the anxious knowledge of a troubled conscience. They had gathered there in John of Wetherby's darkness and now even Arnold's own, triumphant memory seemed tarnished: the memory of that marvellous moment when, in that darkness, he had first touched evidence of the work of a man who had died in Yorkshire, six hundred years ago.